COWBOY
UNDER SIEGE

BY
GAIL BARRETT

Gail Barrett always knew she'd be a writer. Then one day, she discovered a Mills & Boon® novel in a bookstore —and knew she was destined to write romance. Her books have won numerous awards, including a National Readers' Choice Award and Romance Writers of America's prestigious Golden Heart.

She currently lives in western Maryland. Readers can contact her through her website, www.gailbarrett.com.

To John, my own Montana hero.

Acknowledgments:

I'd like to thank the following people for their extraordinary help with this book: Elle Kennedy and Judith Sandbrook for their invaluable input and critiques; René Tanner at Montana State University for explaining how their library system works; Caroline Sullivan and Dorothy Archer for their nursing help; Russ Howe, for information on pharmaceutical companies; Rebecca May-Henson and Mary Jo Archer for patiently answering my questions about horses and bloat; Piper Rome and John K. Barrett for information about weapons. Please note that any mistakes are definitely my own!

And a very special thank-you to Patience Bloom, Keyren Gerlach, and the rest of the Mills & Boon® family for including me in this project. Marie, Beth, Carla, Elle, and Cindy—you ladies rock!

Chapter 1

The sharp report of a gunshot cracked through the afternoon stillness, the echo reverberating through the rolling rangeland and scattering the sparrows on the barbed-wire fence. Cole Kelley jerked up his head and fixed his gaze on the parched brown hills marking the southern boundary of his ranch. Four more shots barked out in quick succession, execution-style. Then a deep, ringing silence gripped the land.

Cole stood dead still, every sense hyperalert, his attention locked on the hills. Nothing moved. No wisp of dust blurred the cloudless sky. Only the dried grass rippled and bowed, paying homage to the perpetual Montana wind.

But coming close on the heels of his sister's abduction, those shots could only mean one thing—trouble.

His pulse kicked into a sprint.

Cole released his hold on his fencing pliers, yanked off his leather work gloves and tugged the cell phone from the back pocket of his jeans. He speed dialed the bunkhouse, relieved he could pick up a signal on the twelve-thousand-acre ranch.

"I just heard gunfire," he said when one of his ranch hands, Earl Runningcrane, answered the phone. "I'm in the south section along Honey Creek. Who've we got working nearby?"

"Nobody. They're all in the northeast section, stacking the rest of the hay."

Just as he'd expected. *Then who had fired shots on his land?*

"All right," he said. "I'm going to investigate. Stand by in case I need help."

A profound sense of uneasiness unfurling inside him, Cole gathered up his fencing tools and whistled softly for Mitzy, the border collie chasing rabbits nearby. He loped through the grass to his pickup truck, the tension that had dogged him for the past two weeks ratcheting higher yet.

There was an outside chance those shots had come from a hunter, but deer season didn't start for another week. And with the danger currently stalking his family...

Cole yanked open the truck door, waited a heartbeat for the dog to leap inside, then slid in beside her and turned the key. "Hold on," he warned as she pointed her nose out the open passenger side window to scent the breeze. "We're moving out fast."

He shifted into gear and gunned the engine, causing the pickup to fishtail on the gravel road. Then he stomped his boot to the floorboard and sped toward the Bar Lazy K's southern boundary, giving rise to a billowing plume of dust.

Those shots could be a coincidence—someone shooting at targets, local teens fooling around. But Cole's gut warned him that he wasn't going to like what he found.

Ever since his father's infidelities had hit the tabloids, creating a national media sensation, his family had been under siege.

Dealing with the press was annoying enough. Reporters tramped over Cole's land for a glimpse of the senator. Paparazzi massed outside the ranch gates like flies over roadkill, their numbers swelling every time another of Hank's mistresses came to light—six so far, proving his father had ignored his wedding vows as easily as he'd forgotten his kids. Photographers had even hovered over the house in helicopters, vying for a shot they could sell to the tabloids, until Cole took out a restraining order to stop them from terrifying the cows.

But there was a darker, far more sinister element seeking his father, unknown enemies who'd threatened his life. And two weeks ago, in a bid to force the senator out of hiding, they'd abducted Cole's sister, Lana, throwing the family into a panic and dramatically upping the stakes.

His jaw clenched tight at the thought of his kidnapped sister, Cole sped up the hill at the corner of his ranch. At the top he hit the brakes, waited for the dust to clear, then scanned the surrounding terrain. Antelope watched from a rise in the distance. Gnarled fence posts stood at the edge of his property like sentinels against the cobalt-blue sky. The gravel road ribboned across the hills toward the Absaroka Mountains, the wide-open rangeland giving way to clusters of pines.

There wasn't a person or vehicle in sight.

His nerves taut, Cole leaped from the truck, grabbed his rifle from the gun rack behind his seat, and chambered a round. Then, keeping Mitzy beside him, he waded through the grass toward the fence. The wind bore down, carrying with it the faint sound of lowing cows.

He reached his barbed-wire fence, and Honey Creek

came into view below him, a sparkling streak meandering through his neighbor's unmowed alfalfa fields. *Still nothing.* His heart beating fast, he ran his gaze over the treeless hillsides, then turned his attention to the grass trampled down around the gate. Someone had recently been here, but who?

The foreboding inside him increasing, he unhooked the barbed wire gate and dragged it aside, then followed the line of crushed grass to the slope of the hill. He swept his gaze to the river bottom where he'd pastured his cattle—stalling on three black cows lying motionless in the sun.

He curled his hands. Anger flared inside him like a wildfire on a brush-choked hill. Someone had deliberately slaughtered his cattle. *But why?*

Furious at the senseless loss, he searched the grass around his feet and found a brass casing glinting in the sun. He examined the markings—300 RUM. Powerful enough to take down big game—or several defenseless cows.

Struggling to control his temper, he stormed down the hill, scanning the slopes for the remainder of his herd. Insects buzzed in the midday heat. The warm wind brushed his face. He glanced upriver and finally caught a glimpse of the scattered cows. They'd crashed through the barbed-wire fence and crossed the creek into his neighbor's alfalfa. Now he had to chase them out before they died of bloat.

Disgusted, he tugged out his cell phone and called the bunkhouse again. "It's me," he said when Earl picked up. "We've got several dead cows."

"Someone *shot* them?"

"Yeah." And then the coward had run away. "The rest of the herd broke through the fence and got into Del Harvey's alfalfa. I need several men here fast. Have them bring extra barbed wire and stomach tubes, just in case. And tell Kenny to bring the front loader to haul away the dead cows."

"Kenny went to the Bozeman airport," his ranch hand said. "He's picking up Rusty's daughter. She's flying in from Chicago for a couple of weeks."

The muscles of Cole's stomach tightened. *Bethany Moore.* This was all he needed. He swore and closed his eyes. But Bethany was no longer his business. Their affair had ended years ago.

"You there, boss?" the cowboy asked.

"Yeah, I'm here." Cole blew out his breath and massaged his eyes. "Just make sure someone brings the front loader. And call the sheriff, Wes Colton. I want him to take a look at this."

Cole disconnected the call, determined to keep his mind off Bethany and the past. She'd made her choices. She'd left Montana. *She'd left him.* But he hadn't expected anything else. He'd learned early in life that people never stayed. The only thing he could depend on was his land.

Turning his thoughts firmly back to his herd, he returned to his truck, placed his rifle in the gun rack, and climbed into the cab. He had to work quickly to drive the surviving cattle back across the creek. Mitzy could keep them safely corralled until the men repaired the fence.

Still furious, he cranked the engine. He glanced in his rearview mirror, waited until Mitzy jumped into the open truck bed, then steered his pickup off the road. He bumped and jostled across the field and through the gate, still barely able to keep his temper in check.

He didn't understand this senseless destruction. And he sure as hell didn't need it. Not when his foreman had broken his leg, leaving him shorthanded. Not when his sister had been abducted and the FBI didn't have any leads. And not when he was smack in the middle of the fall roundup, when the future of the Bar Lazy K Ranch—and the livelihood of a dozen men—depended on him getting a thousand healthy cattle to market in the next two weeks. An entire year of work boiled down to this single paycheck, and every cow, every pound they gained or lost, could make or break the ranch.

He splashed the truck through the shallow creek bed and drove up the opposite bank. Even worse, he still had a hundred head stranded in the mountains he leased for summer pasture. He needed to hightail it up there to rescue them before the predicted snowstorm moved in, instead of wasting time hauling dead cows.

Scowling, he steered around the trio of carcasses, appalled again by the pointless waste. And fierce resolve hardened inside him, an iron vise gripping his gut. He'd put up with the paparazzi. He'd put up with his self-absorbed father and his bodyguards hanging around. But this was different. This was personal, a direct assault on his ranch.

But whoever had done this had underestimated him badly. The Bar Lazy K meant everything to Cole. This ranch was what he did, who he was. It wasn't just his livelihood, it was his soul. And anyone trying to harm it had better watch out. Because if they wanted war, they'd get it.

But he intended to win.

"What do you mean, she *died?*" Bethany Moore stood at the luggage carousel at the Bozeman airport, her cell phone pressed to her ear. "How? When? She was fine last night when I gave her the evening dose." Her seventy-year-old patient had been smiling, showing off photos of her granddaughter. How could she have suddenly died?

"They're looking into it," Adam Kopenski, the lead

doctor administering the trial, said. "I'll let you know what I hear."

"Poor Mrs. Bolter. Her poor family." A lump thickened Bethany's throat. "I'll come right back. I'll have to check the flights, but I'm sure I can get there by tomorrow morning."

"There's no point returning," Adam said. "There's nothing you can do here. The hospital is looking into it, and I can answer any questions they have."

"I know, but—"

"Bethany, forget it. I told you, I've got everything under control. There's no reason for you to come back."

Bethany sighed. Adam was right, but she still felt torn. As head nurse in the drug trial, the patients' safety was her chief concern. "All right, but promise you'll call as soon as you hear anything. Day or night. Don't worry about the time difference."

"I will. And try not to worry. I'm sure it's just one of those things. Now enjoy your vacation. Eat some buffalo burgers and relax."

She forced a smile, trying not to think of Frances Bolter's kind blue eyes. "It's beef on a cattle ranch. Not buffalo."

"Whatever. Just have fun. You work too hard. And I promise I'll keep you informed."

"Thanks, Adam." She meant it. She owed her friend big-time. Not only had he put in a good word for her, helping get her appointed head nurse on the study—a huge advance to her career—but his lively wit had kept her entertained on many a lonely night.

But despite Adam's reassurance, she couldn't put the woman out of her mind. She clicked off her phone and stuck it in her purse just as her hunter-green suitcase pushed through the carousel's plastic flaps. She couldn't imagine what had gone wrong. The Preston-Werner Clinic had a stellar reputation. Adam had screened the patients meticulously for the trials. And Bethany's fellow nurses were all top-notch.

She sighed and pressed her fingertips to her eyes, gritty from the 3:00 a.m. wake-up to make her flight. Adam was right, though. There wasn't much she could do about Mrs. Bolter's death now. And she wasn't naive. She'd lost an occasional patient during the years she'd been a nurse. Still, it was never easy, especially with a patient that sweet.

Besides, her father needed her here in Montana, even if he'd insisted he was all right. He'd fallen off his horse and broken his leg—not an easy injury to recover from at sixty-eight years of age.

Her suitcase began to draw closer. Bethany skirted a man in cowboy boots, hefted it from the carousel, and wheeled it across the luggage-claim area to the tall glass doors. Once outside, she blinked in the afternoon sunshine, Bethany walked past the stone pillars to the end of the sidewalk where she stopped to wait for her ride.

Relax, Adam had told her. She inhaled, filling her lungs with the dry mountain air, and willed her tension to ease—not hard to do since Bozeman's small regional airport had none of the frenzy of O'Hare. There were no shuttle buses spewing exhaust, no constant stream of traffic, no frantic people rushing to catch their flights—just a deserted parking lot dotted with rental cars and an occasional passenger strolling past.

She scanned the mountains ringing the horizon—the Bridger Mountains to the north, the Madison front of the Rockies to the west—their huge peaks dusted with snow. It always amazed her how far she could see out west without humidity hazing the air. Looking up, she spotted a lone hawk riding the currents, and a soothing peace settled inside. She loved the wide open spaces of the land where she'd grown up.

Then a man drove past in a pickup truck and shot her a hostile glare. She stiffened, trying not to let it affect her, but her fleeting sense of harmony disappeared. That right there was the reason she'd moved back east—because of people like him. To them, she was a Native American first, an individual second. Even having a Caucasian mother hadn't helped her fit in. At least in the anonymity of Chicago, she had the freedom to be herself.

And frankly, there'd been nothing to hold her here after high school. No family, aside from her father. No man, not after Cole Kelley made it clear where his priorities lay.

Her stomach turned over at the thought of Cole. In the past she'd managed to avoid him during her visits home to Maple Cove—but that was before her father had become the foreman on his ranch. Now that her father lived in a cabin on the Bar Lazy K, she was bound to run into Cole.

But maybe not. October was roundup time, the busiest time of the year. Cole would be loading cattle, shipping them to market. If she was lucky, she'd never see him around.

And if she did… So what? Cole was ancient history. He'd made his choice—his land over her—and she no longer cared. She had a great life in Chicago—a cozy apartment, good friends, a fabulous job despite the current setback. If she'd hoped for more at one time—if she'd longed for a family and marriage to Cole—she'd learned the futility of that. There was no point dreaming for things she couldn't have.

A new Ford pickup pulled up to the curb, and she waved to the driver, Kenny Greene, a former high school classmate and a cowboy on Cole's ranch. Determined to forget Cole—and her worries in Chicago—she tossed her suitcase into the back of the shiny pickup and climbed into the passenger seat.

For the next two weeks she was on vacation. She would bake her father chokecherry pies, sit on his porch swing and read and go for long rides on his horse while he napped. The Bar Lazy K had twelve thousand acres to get lost in, more if she rode onto government land. She'd never see Cole Kelley or even give him another thought.

She hoped.

Late that evening, Cole pulled into his yard and parked in the fluorescent halo pooling from the pole light next to the barn. More light poured from the ranch house, glinting from the floor-to-ceiling windows like honeyed-gold.

He cut the engine, a deep weariness seeping through his bones, and sighed. Damn, he was tired. He'd put in another sixteen-hour day. He tossed his leather work gloves onto the dashboard and massaged his throbbing temples, still unable to believe that he'd lost those cows.

It made no sense. None of his neighbors would have done it. They were all on friendly terms. In fact, the neighbor who owned the alfalfa was trying to sell Cole his thousand-acre spread—if Cole could swing the down payment when he sold his cows.

And he couldn't imagine his father's mistresses shooting the cattle. Shooting Hank, definitely. Cole was surprised his mother hadn't done that years ago. But to kill the cows?

Still, he'd bet his ranch the killings were related to his father. He couldn't prove it, but given the problems plaguing his family, no other explanation fit.

His back aching, Cole climbed out of the truck and rotated his stiff shoulders, then bent to pet Domino, who'd joined Mitzy in circling his feet. He'd reported the shooting to the sheriff. He'd herded the surviving cows back into their pasture and strung new wire on the fence. And tomorrow, he'd have his men check every cow on every inch of the twenty-square-mile ranch.

He just hoped he could get those cattle to market before that predicted cold front moved in—or anything else went wrong.

A soft whine drew his gaze. "Hey, Ace." He stooped and scratched the gray-muzzled, fifteen-year-old border collie who thumped his tail and licked his hand. Ace had retired from chasing cows when his eyesight failed and now spent his days in the house, pampered by the ranch's cook and housekeeper, Hannah Brown. But, retired or not, the old dog still faithfully greeted Cole whenever he came home.

The other two dogs, not to be ignored, leaped against Cole and butted his hand. Cole laughed and ruffled their fur. When he straightened, they bounded off, heading for their food bowls, no doubt.

His own stomach growled, and he shot a longing glance at the ranch house, wanting nothing more than a cold beer, a hot meal and some long-overdue oblivion in his king-size bed. But he had a lame colt to check on first.

He strode to the barn, the sight of the freshly painted corral easing his tension a notch. His grandmother had built the lavish ranch house on the family homestead, its soaring ceilings and two-story windows more suited to Aspen than Maple Cove. But the barn... Fierce satisfaction surged inside him. That was Cole's contribution, the first thing he'd remodeled when he and his brother Dylan had bought the place. He'd added a dozen horse stalls, created more heated space to birth calves. He'd also upgraded the pens and loading chutes, satisfied that he now had a modern outfit to tend his stock.

He opened the wide barn door, greeted by the familiar

scent of hay. A soft light came from the nearest stall where his ranch foreman kept his horse.

"Rusty?" he called out, his exasperation rising. The stubborn man was supposed to be lying in bed with his broken leg propped up, not fooling around with his horse.

He swung open the gate to the stall, expecting to see his old foreman hobbling on his crutches and cast. Instead, a woman stood with her back to him, brushing Rusty's chestnut mare.

Bethany Moore. Cole abruptly came to a stop. Even after a dozen years, the sight of her straight black hair shimmering in the lamp light and those long, slender legs in her tight blue jeans knocked his heart off course.

She whipped around, and her black, fathomless eyes met his, giving his pulse an erratic beat. He scanned her full, sultry lips, her high, exotic cheekbones, the feminine curves of her breasts. And damned if she didn't still get to him, even after all these years. From her dusky skin and erotic mouth to the intelligence in her sooty eyes, she called to something inside him, appealing to him in a visceral, primitive way.

And memories flashed back before he could stop them—Bethany riding beside him into the mountains, her satiny hair streaming behind her like a sensual flag. Bethany digging with him for arrowheads, her white teeth flashing as she laughed. Bethany poised above him, her tawny skin bathed by moonlight as they made love beneath the stars.

As a teenager, she'd burned him alive. She'd sparked a craving in him he couldn't resist. And he'd never experienced anything remotely like it since.

Realizing he was already half aroused, he scowled. After the day he'd had, Bethany was the last person he needed to deal with. "What are you doing here?" he said, his voice roughened by fatigue.

Her full mouth flattened. She flicked her head, swinging her long, straight hair over her back. "Brushing my father's horse."

Obviously. His frown deepened. She lifted her chin, her eyes sparking fire, a sure indication that he'd ticked her off. Then she hung up the brush on a peg in the stall and pushed past him out the door, her soft scent curling around him like a taunt. "Bethany…"

She spun around. "I'm only here to take care of my father, okay? I'm not going to bother you."

The hell she wouldn't. Just seeing her stirred up feelings he didn't want to deal with, memories he had no desire to relive. His temples suddenly pounding, he crossed his arms. "I was just surprised to see you. I never expected you to come back to Maple Cove, considering how anxious you were to leave."

"Anxious?" She shot him an incredulous look. "I had no choice. You knew I couldn't stay here."

She meant she *wouldn't* stay. But no one ever did. His own temper rising, he lifted one shoulder in a shrug. "It was none of my business what you did."

"Yes, you made that clear." She shook her head, and a weary look replaced the temper in her eyes. "Don't worry, Cole. I'm only here for the next two weeks. I'll be sure to stay out of your way." She turned on her heel and stalked from the barn, her boots rapping the cement floor.

He watched her go, a dull ache battering his skull. *Hell.* He'd screwed that up royally, putting the perfect cap on an already lousy day.

He pinched the bridge of his nose and exhaled. He hadn't meant to hurt her feelings. And he hadn't meant to dredge up the past. She'd just caught him off guard. He was exhausted, hungry, worried about his ranch and his sister. He'd needed time to prepare.

But maybe it was for the best if she was mad. He didn't need more complications in his life—and she'd only leave again. Besides, they weren't exactly friends, despite the attraction he still felt. They were former classmates, former lovers…former everything. Whatever they'd shared was over, and there was nothing left to say.

Nothing except *sorry*. He dragged his hand over his face with a sigh. He owed her an apology, all right. No matter what his mood, she hadn't deserved to have her head chewed off. But he'd deal with that in the morning.

And then he'd stay as far from Bethany—and temptation—as he could.

Chapter 2

So much for not giving Cole Kelley another thought.

Bethany stood in the pharmacy in the neighboring town of Honey Creek the following morning, berating her lack of control. She'd spent the entire night tossing and turning, reliving every nuance of that strained encounter in the barn. She'd overreacted. She'd let Cole's vibrant blue eyes demolish her composure, bringing back a flood of rejection and pain. But she hadn't expected to see him so soon—or that he'd look so impossibly good.

Disgusted with herself, she exhaled, determined not to spend more time thinking about Cole. If she'd learned anything in the years since high school, it was that there were things she couldn't change. So she'd moved on. She'd made a good life for herself in Chicago. And she had enough to worry about without obsessing over him.

"I've got it in stock," the pharmacist said, returning to the counter where she waited. "But it will be about twenty minutes before I can get to it."

"That's fine." Pulling her mind back to her father's prescription, Bethany glanced at her watch. "I'll do some shopping and come back."

Dead tired from the lack of sleep, she strolled up the narrow aisle of the pharmacy and pushed open the door to the street. It was early, barely nine o'clock, and nothing else was open in Honey Creek except the ranch supply store and Kelley's Cookhouse, the town's most popular place to eat.

Yawning, she glanced up the empty main street toward the restaurant, debating whether to get some coffee while she waited for the prescription. She could definitely use the caffeine boost. But Cole's aunt and uncle owned the cookhouse, and she'd gone there on dates with Cole—memories she didn't need to stir up.

Another yawn convinced her. She started up the tree-lined sidewalk just as a black, four-wheel-drive pickup pulled up to the restaurant and parked. Cole Kelley climbed out, and Bethany came to a halt.

Her heart somersaulted as he turned toward her. Their eyes met in the morning sunshine, and her traitorous pulse began to race. She shifted her weight, the urge to flee surging inside her, but she forced herself to stay put. She wasn't going to spend the next two weeks bolting like a startled rabbit whenever she ran into Cole.

He started toward her, his long, determined strides devouring the distance between them. She pasted a neutral expression on her face, refusing to let him see how rattled she felt. But it was hard to feign indifference when the lanky, rangy teen she'd once loved had turned into an impossibly virile man.

She skimmed the wide, thick planks of his shoulders, the intriguing fit of his faded jeans. Years of ranch work had broadened his neck and back, erasing any hint of softness, turning his powerful biceps to steel.

She swallowed around the dust in her throat, her blood humming as he drew near. Cole had certainly aged nicely. And he was no vain Chicago businessman with muscles toned in front of a mirror. He was the real deal, a rugged Montana cowboy, a one-hundred-percent-natural male.

He stopped close enough to touch her, and his startling blue eyes captured hers. Her pulse beating wildly, she scanned his sensual mouth, the strong angles of his rock hard jaw, the lean, tanned planes of his face. Sunshine slanted through the branches of a nearby maple, highlighting the sun kissed streaks in his espresso-colored hair.

"Listen, Bethany…" His deep voice rumbled through her, and she rubbed her arms, trying to quell her response. He had the sexiest voice she'd ever heard, a deep, gravelly rasp that tempted a woman to sin. And when he'd whispered to her in the dark…

She shivered again, battling her reaction. It was conditioning, nothing more, like Pavlov's dogs. One look at Cole and she instantly thought of sex—which was inevitable, considering the molten affair they'd had.

But she knew that wasn't quite accurate. Any woman would react to him the same way. Cole's blatant masculinity attracted women like a lone tree drew lightning during a violent electrical storm.

"I'm sorry if I was rude last night," he continued. His lips edged into a grimace, making sexy dents bracket his mouth, and she found it hard to breathe. "I had a bad day. I didn't mean to take it out on you."

"That's all right."

"No, it's not. Not really." His intense eyes skewered hers. "How about if we start over? I'll buy you a cup of coffee."

"Oh." Her gaze shot to Kelley's Cookhouse, where two elderly ranchers limped out the door. "Thanks, but I don't think—"

"Come on, I owe you that much. And you can fill me in on Rusty's progress." He tilted his head. "I was heading there anyway. I need to talk to my Uncle Don."

Her instincts warned against it, but she never did have any willpower around Cole. A whispered word, one glance from those hypnotic eyes had convinced her to abandon every inhibition—with the most erotic results.

But that was then. Surely she could have a cup of coffee with him now without falling apart. And maybe it would put their relationship on a more casual footing. Then she could simply nod and wave when she saw him on the ranch—and *finally* get him out of her head.

"All right. Coffee it is." She just hoped she wasn't making a mistake.

"So how is Rusty?" Cole asked, adjusting his longer stride to hers.

"He's in a lot of pain. He won't admit it, but I heard him groaning all night." While she was lying awake thinking about Cole. "That's why I'm here. The pharmacy in Maple Cove didn't have his prescription and I didn't want to wait another day."

"It was a nasty break."

And an even odder accident. "He didn't tell me what happened, just that he fell off his horse." Which was bizarre. She's seen her father stick to the back of unbroken mustangs. She couldn't imagine him getting thrown from his steady mare.

"He was out riding fences in the pasture that borders Rock Creek, near the old Blackfoot teepee ring. He'd stopped there on his way back up to the mountains to find my missing cows. He said his mare spooked and dragged him a ways."

"Dragged him?" Horrified, Bethany stopped and gaped at Cole. "He didn't tell me that."

"He probably didn't want you to worry."

Or insist he stay off a horse, especially at his age. But she knew better than to suggest it. Behind her father's quiet, laid-back facade lurked fierce stubbornness and pride.

"I can't believe his horse dragged him. That mare never spooks. What on earth set her off?"

"He didn't see," Cole said as they resumed walking.

"He's lucky he wasn't killed." Shaken that she could have lost him, Bethany climbed the wooden steps to the cookhouse. While she'd been oblivious in Chicago, her father could have died.

Cole pulled open the door, jangling the welcoming cowbell, and she preceded him inside. The restaurant hadn't changed in the past twelve years. The same red-checkered cloths still covered the tables. The old, planked bar still dominated the room, flanked by square wooden stools. Cattle brands and horseshoes decorated the walls, along with photos from local rodeos. The familiar scents of coffee and bacon permeated the air.

She didn't know how many hours she'd spent here in high school, hanging around with Cole. But it brought back a rush of longing, a poignant reminder of the hopes she'd left behind.

A reminder she *definitely* didn't need right now. She was trying to gain some distance from Cole, not remember the good times they'd shared.

The saloon-style doors to the kitchen swung open. Cole's aunt Bonnie Gene came bustling out, her face wreathed around a smile. "Why, Bethany Moore! Aren't you a sight for sore eyes." She hurried around the bar, her shoulder-length brown hair swinging, her light brown eyes shining with warmth, and Bethany couldn't help but smile back.

"It's about time you came back here," Bonnie Gene scolded. "And aren't you as gorgeous as ever!" She gave her a hard hug and turned to Cole. "Isn't she gorgeous, Cole?"

Bethany's face burned. She braved a look at Cole. His eyes met hers, and a sudden sizzle of awareness stopped her breath. *So he still felt it, too.*

"Yeah," he said, his voice gruff. "She's gorgeous."

Her heart skittering, she jerked her gaze away.

"Sit right here." Bonnie Gene ushered her onto a stool. She pulled another seat close and pushed Cole into it, maneuvering him faster than a border collie herding cows. "Coffee?" she asked Bethany.

Still struggling to regain her composure, Bethany managed to nod. "Sure, I—"

"Don't you dare move. I'll get Donald and be right back."

Bonnie Gene rushed off. Cole's thigh bumped hers, putting Bethany's nerves on further alert. "I see she hasn't changed," she said in the suddenly awkward silence.

"Yeah. Sorry about that." He rose, dragged his stool a foot away, and she battled back a sliver of hurt. But he was right to put some space between them. Bonnie Gene was a notorious matchmaker—and the last thing Bethany wanted was to encourage her. This was just coffee between old friends, not the rekindling of their high-school romance.

Then the kitchen doors sprang open and Cole's uncle came out, accompanied by Bonnie Gene. Donald had added a few pounds to his midsection over the years, but his friendly blue eyes hadn't changed. And he still wore his short, white hair in that oddly lopsided style, which gave the renowned businessman a deceptively guileless look. "Bethany, it's good to see you again."

"It's nice to be here." She realized, with surprise, that it was true. In Chicago, she was always surrounded by strangers, an anonymity and freedom she liked. Still, there was something comforting about running into people she knew.

Bonnie Gene filled their cups with steaming coffee. "Now tell me, how is your father doing?"

"Not great," Bethany admitted. "He's in a lot of pain. That's why I'm here, to fill his prescription."

Bonnie Gene clucked. "A man his age shouldn't be on a horse."

"Can't keep him off it," Cole said, his deep voice rumbling through her nerves.

"That's right," Don cut in, sounding belligerent. "A man's got a right to live his life the way he wants no matter how old he gets."

Bethany sipped her coffee to hide a smile. Everyone knew that Bonnie Gene kept her husband on a short leash, especially when it came to his beloved cigars.

Bonnie Gene rolled her eyes at her husband and turned to Cole. "And how about Hank? How's he doing?"

Cole made a sound of disgust. "The same. Still hiding in the house, leaving the rest of us to deal with his mess."

Bethany stole a glance at Cole's handsome profile, a reluctant spurt of sympathy twisting inside. She'd heard about the senator's infidelities. His mistresses had been popping up like gophers in a hay field, dominating the tabloids for weeks. And the media was having a field day, relishing the California senator's spectacular fall from grace—especially given the "family values" platform on which he'd built his career.

She could imagine how the scandal affected Cole. Hank had been a lousy, self-centered father from the get-go, ignoring his wife and children to pursue his political career. His absence and indifference had wounded Cole deeply, turning the neglected child into a wild and rebellious teen—until his desperate mother had sent him to Montana to live with his Uncle Don.

Donald and Bonnie Gene's patience had subdued Cole's anger. The rugged Montana land had given him a reason to live. Now just when Cole had put his life together, his father had come back—creating havoc Cole surely didn't need.

"Has he told you any more about what's going on?" Bonnie Gene asked him.

Cole shook his head, the furrow deepening between his dark brows. "I was hoping he'd said something to you."

"You mean about La—" Bonnie Gene glanced at Bethany and clamped her hand over her lips. The men exchanged uneasy looks, and a strained silence fell over the group.

There was something they didn't want her to know.

Bethany pretended to study her coffee, experiencing a sudden feeling of hurt—which was ridiculous. Cole had no reason to confide in her. She hadn't been part of his life in years.

"About anything," Cole finally said. "You heard that someone shot three of my cows?"

"*Shot* them?" Bethany snapped her gaze to Cole. "Are you serious?"

He nodded, his grim gaze shifting to hers. "I found them by Honey Creek."

Bethany's heart tripped. Another wave of sympathy surged inside. That ranch meant everything to Cole. He'd slaved for years to buy it with Dylan, working with a single-minded intensity, sacrificing everything for the land—even his relationship with her.

His uncle leaned on the counter. "You called the sheriff?"

"Yeah. Wes Colton came out to look, but there wasn't much for him to go on. I doubt it's a coincidence, though. All this trouble started when my father showed up. That's why I was hoping he'd talked to you."

Donald's face flushed. "No, he hasn't called me."

Bonnie Gene turned to her husband and frowned. "Then why haven't you called him?"

"Why should I?"

"He's your brother, your family. And he needs you, no matter what he did in the past."

Cole grunted. "Family or not, I wish he'd go hide somewhere else. Bad enough I've got the paparazzi tramping through my fields, leaving the gates unlocked. Now I've got someone killing my cows."

"That's not Hank's fault." Bonnie Gene topped off Bethany's coffee. "Not that he's a saint—not by a long shot. What he did to your mother and you kids…" She pursed her lips in distaste. "He deserves to be horsewhipped for that. But no one is all good or all bad, not even Hank."

She turned to her frowning husband. "And you need to forget your blasted pride for once and talk to him. He's your brother, for Pete's sake. He needs your help."

Donald's expression turned mulish. "He can call me if he wants to talk. I have nothing to say to him. Now I need to check on the food." He pushed through the swinging doors to the kitchen and disappeared.

"Stubborn man," Bonnie Gene muttered under her breath.

Bethany took a swallow of coffee. Cole's father was a piece of work, all right. He'd alienated his wife and children, and had been estranged from his half brother, Donald, for years. Now even his mistresses appeared fed up.

The soft chimes of a cell phone interrupted her thoughts. Cole reached back, the motion showcasing the impressive definition in his biceps, and pulled his phone from the back pocket of his jeans. He frowned at the display. "I'd better take this."

He rose and walked a few steps away. His broad shoulders stiffened, and Bethany knew instantly that the news was bad. "How many?" he asked, his deep voice clipped. "All right. I'll be right there."

He slipped the phone back into his pocket and turned to face them, tension vibrating off his muscled frame. "I've got to go. Someone dammed up Rock Creek, just above the northeast pasture, cutting off water to the cows."

Bethany's heart squeezed. Without water, cattle died fast. "Are they—"

"I don't know how many we've lost yet. No one has checked that pasture since your dad got hurt, so they might have gone without water for several days." He angled his chin toward the bar. "Sorry to run."

"Don't be silly. You've got more important things to do than sit here and talk to me."

"Yes, go on," Bonnie Gene urged him. "Just let us know what we can do to help."

He nodded, his mind obviously elsewhere, then strode across the wooden floor to the door. He flung the door open, making the cowbell clank, and stomped across the porch outside.

Filled with compassion, Bethany watched him go. He'd be torn up about the suffering animals and furious that someone had attacked his ranch—not to mention angry at the financial loss.

"He's a good man," Bonnie Gene said, echoing her thoughts. "And a lonely one. He just needs the right woman to soften him up."

Warning bells clanged. Bethany swiveled back to Bonnie Gene, determined to nip that train of thought. "Don't look at me. Cole and I are old friends, nothing more."

"Of course. I know that." Bonnie Gene gave her an innocent look. She pulled a small photo album from her apron pocket, set it on the bar, and flipped it open, turning it so Bethany could see. "You haven't seen my granddaughter yet. Eve's daughter, Patience. My little angel is four months old."

A darling, red-haired baby girl smiled up at her, softening Bethany's heart. "Oh, my. What a doll." She slowly flipped through the pages, remembering when she'd dreamed of forever with Cole.

She straightened, shocked at the direction of her thoughts. She had no future with Cole. He'd never marry her, no matter what his aunt believed—a lesson she'd learned years ago.

And no way could she delude herself—because that would only bring pain. It had taken her years to get over him the first time, years to resign herself to harsh reality and finally move on with her life.

And no matter how cute Bonnie Gene's granddaughter was, no matter how much Cole still made her pulse pound, she couldn't succumb to dreams.

She was older now. Definitely wiser. And she would only be here for two short weeks. She had to keep her emotional distance, not allow herself to get swept up in Cole's problems and begin to care.

Because that was a surefire path to heartbreak—an experience she refused to repeat.

* * *

Determined to hold fast to that resolution, Bethany drove through the towering log entrance to the Bar Lazy K Ranch an hour later and headed to her father's house. The main ranch buildings were clustered around a large, grassy triangle a quarter mile in from the gate. The barn, workshops and machinery sheds formed one end of the complex. In another corner stood the foreman's log cabin, where her father currently lived, with the ranch hands' bunkhouse beyond that. Cole's house—a lavish, two-story stone building with floor-to-ceiling windows—stood apart from the other buildings, taking advantage of the mountain views.

She parked the truck beside her father's cabin, then got out and glanced around. Several men worked near the machinery shed, loading a backhoe onto a flatbed trailer. Others strapped shovels to four-wheelers, preparing to deal with the dammed-up stream. She didn't see Cole, but his truck was parked by the tractors, so she assumed he was still around.

She climbed the wooden porch steps, her father's prescription in hand. Then she hesitated by the porch swing and took another look at the men. Even from a distance she could feel their tension, which was easy to understand. Ranchers worked hard under tough conditions—from winter blizzards reaching forty below to sweltering summer heat. Seeing their work destroyed would infuriate them.

Troubled, she pulled open the door and went inside. Her father sat reading the newspaper in a recliner near the window, his broken leg propped up, his crutches lying beside him on the braided rug.

"Hi, Dad." She bent and kissed his leathered cheek, careful not to bump his bruises and scrapes. "I've got your pain medication. Have you had breakfast? You want me to scramble you some eggs?"

"I can do it," he grumbled. "I don't need you to wait on me."

"I know that." She stifled a sigh, remembering Bonnie Gene's comment about stubborn men. "But since I'm up..."

"Fine." He set his paper aside. "But just get me one of the sandwiches Hannah brought by. She put them in the fridge."

"All right." Still thinking about Cole's cattle, Bethany entered the kitchen and took the medicine out of the bag. Maple Cove had its share of crime—domestic disputes, meth labs, occasional thefts. But to deliberately destroy someone's livelihood...

Incredulous, she shook out a pill, then went to the sink to fill a glass from the tap. Above the sink the white lace curtains fluttered around the open window, framing a view of the old-fashioned clothesline in the small backyard. That was Maple Cove—sheets drying in the sunshine, kids playing baseball in their grassy yards—not cold-blooded killings and sabotage.

Still unable to believe it, she returned to the living room with the pill. "Here you go. Take this while I get your food."

He leaned away. "I don't want to be all drugged up."

"It's only for a couple of days until the worst of the pain is gone. You need to rest," she added when he opened his mouth to argue. "I heard you thrashing around all night." She set the glass on the side table and handed him the pill.

"Since when did you get so bossy?" he muttered but dutifully gulped it down.

Leaving him to his morning newspaper, she crossed the wooden floor to the kitchen and readied his food. But his comment sparked a sliver of guilt. She didn't visit her widowed father as often as she should. And he was getting older; his thinning white hair proved that. But she led a busy life in Chicago and could rarely get away.

Still feeling guilty, she put the sandwich on a plate and carried it out. She rearranged her father's pillows, making sure he was comfortable, then sat on the adjacent couch. It wasn't just his advancing age that bothered her, but that she'd lost touch with the everyday happenings in his life—his accident, the trouble on Cole's ranch...

"I saw Cole Kelley in town," she said. "Why didn't you tell me your horse dragged you?"

Her father swallowed a bite of sandwich. "It wasn't important."

"How can you say that? You could have been killed. Don't you think I deserved to know?"

"What was the point? There was nothing you could do about it." He returned his attention to his food.

He was right, but she still wished he'd told her. She drummed her fingers on the couch. "So how did it happen? Cole said Red—"

"It was an accident, that's all. So just drop it."

Bethany blinked, shocked by his testy tone. Her father never lost his temper. He was the most even-keeled man she knew. But pain put everyone out of sorts.

She studied his craggy face, the deep lines testament to a lifetime spent working in the wind and sun. "Cole told me about the cattle getting shot," she said, changing the subject. "And now the stream's dammed up."

Her father paused in midbite. His gaze shot to hers. "What stream?"

"Rock Creek. He just found out a little while ago. The cows couldn't get any water. He doesn't know how many head he might have lost." She leaned forward. "You think it

has something to do with his father? Cole said the problems started when the senator showed up."

Her father paled. "I don't know."

"You must have an opinion. You're here every day."

"I said I don't know." Rusty's voice turned defensive.
He scowled and tugged his ear. "How would I when I'm
stuck in here with a broken leg?"

He was lying. The realization barreled through her,
stealing her breath. No one else would have noticed, but
she'd played cards with her father for years—and that pull
to the ear invariably gave him away.

But why would he lie? What could he possibly have to
hide? Surely he wasn't involved in the sabotage. He was
the most honorable man she knew.

Still scowling, he got up, grabbed his crutches and hobbled away. Bethany slumped on the couch, stunned by his
behavior, questions spinning through her mind. Her father
would never harm an animal. And he would never hurt
Cole. It was insane even to have doubts.

But then what was he hiding? Why hadn't he told her
the truth? Was he merely embarrassed about his accident
or something more?

Her thoughts and emotions in turmoil, she rose and
walked to the window and gazed out at the busy men.
One thing was clear. Something bad was happening at the
ranch. And her father might know more than he'd let on.

Cole stalked past on his way to the ranch house, his
broad shoulders rigid with tension, anger quickening his
stride. She hugged her arms, knowing she shouldn't care.
Cole and his ranch weren't her business. She had her own
problems to deal with—namely Mrs. Bolter's death. She
didn't need to worry about Cole.

But as he passed, a sinking feeling settled inside her,
her heart winning the war it waged with her head. She

couldn't just stand here and do nothing. Cole was in trouble, his ranch under attack. And no matter how badly their relationship had ended, it wasn't in her nature to withhold her help.

She stepped away from the window, her mind made up. She'd settle her father down for a nap, then ride his horse to the stream. On the way, she could stop in the pasture where he'd had his accident and search for clues.

If her father *was* hiding something, she would find out.

Chapter 3

Bethany galloped across the field on her father's mare an hour later, the brisk wind brushing her face, a heady sense of exhilaration flooding her veins. The brilliant blue sky soared above her. Wheat-colored grass carpeted the rolling rangeland on every side. Closer to the mountains, hills rose like gnarled fingers, their ancient, glacier-carved valleys shadowed with aspens and pines.

She slowed Red to a walk, her breath coming in ragged gasps, the scent of dried grass filling her lungs. The ever-present wind rustled in the silence—whispers from her ancestors, her father had said. She smiled at the fanciful thought. She'd always loved imagining her father's people traveling through these foothills, hunting for buffalo. They'd seen the same, unchanging scenery that she did, felt the same, unending wind. Even now the sheer magnitude of the wild land awed her, the beauty a balm to her soul.

Pulling herself out of her musings, she angled her hat against the midday sun, then guided the mare toward the fence marking the perimeter of Cole's ranch. She'd detoured on her way to the dammed-up stream, hoping to find the spot where her father's accident had occurred. Although she doubted he had anything to do with Cole's problems, he was lying about something—and she intended to find out what.

Keeping Red to a walk, she scanned the pasture. A gopher scurried by. The western wheat grass bobbed in the wind. She pushed up the sleeves of her long-sleeved T-shirt, growing warm in the sun. But in typical Montana fashion, a storm front was due to arrive any day now, dumping snow on the mountain peaks.

She continued riding along the fence line—past the circle of stones forming the old teepee ring, past a cluster of Black Angus cows. A dozen yards later, she spotted a churned-up section of ground and stopped. Hoof prints and tire tracks crisscrossed the dirt, but they didn't tell her much. It rarely rained this side of the Rockies, so they could have been here for months.

She slowly circled the area, trying to envision how her father's accident had played out—but there were no tree branches to spook the horse, nothing flapping in the wind. She brought Red to a halt with a sigh. She was wasting her time. She wasn't going to miraculously figure this out. She might as well do something useful and go help the men with the cows.

She reined Red around, intending to do just that when something black in the grass caught her eye. "Whoa," she told the mare and leaped down. She walked back and picked it up. It was a strip of leather, an inch wide, maybe fifteen inches long with a braided horsehair inset—a browband from a bridle, she'd guess. Not her father's, though.

He didn't own any showy tack. He'd used the same plain, utilitarian bridles for forty years.

But even if it belonged to another cowboy, what did that prove? Anyone could have dropped it here.

Discouraged, she stuffed the browband into her pocket and mounted the horse. But even without any evidence, she couldn't stifle her doubts. What if the browband *did* mean something? What if her father hadn't come here alone? What if Red hadn't spooked and dragged him? But then how had he broken his leg?

A cloud passed overhead, towing a giant shadow over the earth, and a sudden sense of foreboding chilled her heart. Unsettled, she clucked Red into motion, trying to subdue her unruly thoughts. She couldn't jump to conclusions based solely on a leather scrap. And even if her father had lied to her, so what? He might not be hiding anything bad. He might have withheld the truth out of embarrassment or to keep her from worrying about him.

Moments later she reached Rock Creek, the clear glacial runoff that fed Cole's wells in this part of the ranch. Determined to focus on reality instead of conjectures, she followed the drone of a machine downstream. She skirted a jumble of boulders, passed through the shade of some cottonwood trees, then rounded another bend. When she spotted Cole wrestling a calf to the ground, she brought her horse to a halt.

Dust billowed over the men. Cows bellowed behind them, their frantic cries filling the air. Cole dug his heels into the dirt, flipped the bleating calf to the ground, and Kenny Greene raced over to help him hold it down. A man she didn't recognize crouched beside them, and began examining the suffering calf—Judd Walker, Maple Cove's new veterinarian, no doubt.

Bethany peered through the blowing dust to the

backhoe, then to the corrals where they'd penned the herd. The cows lunged and cried, desperate to break out and quench their thirst. But drinking water too fast would cause their brains to swell, killing even more of the herd.

She glanced farther downstream to the dead cows dotting the bank, and her throat closed at the sight. Who would want to hurt those innocent animals—and why? Cole didn't have enemies that she knew. People liked him in Maple Cove. Sure, he came from a wealthy family, but he'd worked his heart out to buy this ranch—putting in longer hours than his men did, never shirking an unpleasant job. And people respected that.

Her gaze swung back to the busy cowboys. She recognized most of the faces—Bill, Earl Runningcrane, her old classmate Kenny Greene. But there were some new ones, too. The same hollow feeling she'd experienced in the restaurant swirled back, but she forced it aside. So what if the ranch had changed since she'd left? Her life had moved on, too.

The sick calf thrashed, knocking Cole's hat to the ground, and her gaze gravitated to him. He swore, his arm muscles bunching as he held the calf, the veins bulging in his tanned neck.

"Almost done," the vet said. "Just a few more seconds."

Cole grunted, his dark hair dampened with sweat, dirt streaking his hard jaw. And the sheer maleness of him made her heart take a crazy beat.

"Got it," the vet said. Cole nodded at Kenny. They released the calf and leaped away. The calf staggered to his feet, wobbling badly. Cole whistled to Mitzy, who instantly raced over and steered it back into the herd.

Cole wiped his jaw on his sleeve, his T-shirt plastered to his powerful torso. He reached down to grab his hat, causing his faded jeans to tighten on his muscled behind.

Bethany shifted in the saddle, suddenly restless. No matter what had gone wrong between them, Cole was still hands down the most attractive man she'd ever seen. And the thrills she'd felt in his arms…

"Well, look who's back." A cowboy trotted up on a big roan gelding, pulling her attention from Cole.

Tony Whittaker. She recoiled in distaste. As a child, he'd bullied her daily. And as a teen… She suppressed a shudder, refusing to go down that humiliating track. Fortunately, she'd learned that he would ignore her if she refused to show any fear.

"Get out of my way, Tony. I've got work to do." She tugged the reins to the right, intending to go around him, but he shifted his gelding and blocked her way.

"If it's work you want, you can work me over good." His eyes dipped to her chest, his innuendo clear.

Her mouth flattened, disgust churning through her, but she deliberately steadied her voice. "Look, I don't have time for this. Those cows need help. Now get your horse out of my way."

His lips thinned, sudden meanness flashing in his eyes. "A squaw like you would be lucky to have me. I can show you what a real man's like."

Her face burned, fury building inside her at the racial insult, and she tightened her grip on the reins. Idiots like Tony were the reason she'd left Maple Cove. But she bit down an angry retort, knowing better than to take his bait. She refused to cause trouble for Cole.

She nudged Red forward, but Tony moved his gelding closer, and her patience snapped. "What the hell is your problem? I said to get out of my way."

"Why you—"

"Tony!" Cole shouted. "Get over here and give us a hand."

"On my way." Tony shot her an even stare, making the fine hairs rise on the nape of her neck, then wheeled his horse around. Bethany didn't move as he rode off, her hands trembling, anger still pumping through her veins. Then she signaled for Red to get moving and headed downstream to join the men monitoring the thirsty cows.

So Tony was still a creep. That much hadn't changed. She frowned, wondering if he was behind Cole's problems. Killing helpless cows sounded like something he'd do.

But criminal or not, she'd be smart to watch her back. Instead of finding answers, she'd ticked off an old enemy—a dangerous one at that.

She reached the herd, then gave her father's veteran cutting horse free rein. Red sprang into action like a kindergartener let out for recess, charging across the field, dancing back and forth to head off the bolting cows.

But as she worked, her plans for a relaxing vacation crumbled fast. She hadn't found any answers. She still didn't know why her father had lied. But if there was any chance her father's fall was more than a simple accident, she had to find out.

Red pivoted sharply and changed directions, and she spared a glance at Cole. He stood with his feet planted wide, his hat tilted low, his big hands braced on his hips. His gaze connected with hers through the shifting dust, and her heart made a heavy thud.

She had to get answers, all right—which meant she had to stick close to the men. But she was doing this for her father's sake and her own peace of mind—*not* to be around Cole.

She just hoped she'd remember that.

"All right. Listen up," Cole said. He stood on the bank of the stream they'd cleared, waiting for his tired men to gather around. The vet had returned to town an hour earlier. The sheriff had taken his statement and gone. They'd carted the dead cattle to a local food bank and made sure the wells were working again.

His head pounding, he whistled again for his men. Bethany rode to the edge of the group, then leaped off her horse. She'd done an amazing job controlling the cattle, putting his ranch hands to shame. But she'd always been an expert rider. Watching her on a cutting horse was like viewing a work of art.

A fact not lost on the men. Tony hadn't taken his eyes off her all day.

Scowling, he cleared his throat. "I'm sure you've figured out by now that we've got a problem." And he was tired of being caught off guard. "So I'm moving up our schedule. We need to get these calves shipped off before anything else goes wrong."

"I thought the trucks weren't available until next week," Kenny said.

"I'll find some trucks somewhere." *He hoped.* He'd originally planned to ship his cattle to market last week during the round up. But his herd had splintered in the mountains, stranding a hundred head near the divide. He'd rescheduled the trucks, hoping to use the delay to his advantage, getting the calves' weight up while he rescued the rest of the herd. But now, with someone killing his cattle, he couldn't afford to wait.

"First thing in the morning we'll start in the southern section. We also need to start patrolling at night," he added. "I'll draw up a schedule."

The men grumbled. Cole couldn't blame them. They already worked long hours. But what choice did he have? If he lost enough money, the ranch would fold, and they'd all be out of a job.

"If you know anyone looking for work, let me know." He scanned the group, but no one answered. His gaze stalled on Tony, who was staring at Bethany again.

Cole's mood darkened. He didn't care who she dated. He had no claim on her. But he didn't need her distracting the men.

Bethany swung up on the mare and trotted off. Tony vaulted into his saddle a second later, turning his gelding to go in pursuit.

"Tony," he barked. "Take my truck and drive into Maple Cove. Leave word at the bars that we're looking for extra men. Do the same in Honey Creek. I'll ride your horse back to the barn and check fences along the way." He glanced around at the men. "The rest of you get something to eat. I'll bring the schedule by later."

The ranch hands began to disperse. His eyes simmering with resentment, Tony dismounted and handed Cole his gelding's reins. Cole fished his keys from his pocket and tossed them his way. "Tell them I'm paying overtime," he added.

He hoisted himself into the saddle, then took off after Bethany, ignoring the men's speculative looks. He needed to check his fences—nothing more. And if Bethany happened to be riding the same way…

He caught up with her a few minutes later as she climbed the hill. "Thanks for helping today."

Her eyes met his, and a familiar jolt changed the rhythm of his pulse. She'd always had the damnedest effect on him. One glance across the cafeteria in high school, and he'd fallen for her hard.

"I enjoyed it," she said, her throaty voice conjuring up erotic memories he'd tried for years to forget. "It feels good to be on a horse again."

"I'll bet." They'd spent some of their best moments

together on horseback, racing across these hills. He guided the gelding toward the fence, checking the barbed wire for problems as he rode along, but his eyes kept returning to her. A flush tinged her sculpted cheeks. Her straight black hair fluttered against her back. She looked good riding beside him. *Right.*

But she hadn't cared enough about him to stay.

"I'm sorry about the cows," she said.

"Yeah." He shifted his gaze to the land bordering his fence. "I was hoping to turn a profit this year, enough for a down payment on Del Harvey's place."

"He's selling?"

Cole nodded. "He can't make a go of it anymore, not with property taxes so high." Ever since celebrities had discovered the valley, real estate prices had soared.

"How big is his ranch?"

"A thousand acres. The land's good. Lots of native grasses, year-round herds of elk. There's a movement underway to get cattle off federal lands," he explained. "If that goes through I could lose my BLM lease. Del's ranch would provide me with summer pasture, enough so I wouldn't have to reduce my herd." But every dead cow— and dollar lost—jeopardized that plan.

Bethany looked toward the mountains, a small crease bisecting her brow. "How long will he hold on?"

"I don't know. He's been getting calls from developers. They're offering him a lot of money. He wants to keep the ranch intact, but if I don't come up with the down payment soon…"

His chest tight, he scanned the huge granite peaks scraping the sky, the aspens glimmering in the waning sunlight like burnished gold. He inhaled deeply, soaking in the beauty of the land. He couldn't begin to express his feelings for this place. This wild land touched something inside him, giving him a reason to live.

And he'd do everything in his power to preserve it, to make sure future generations could breathe the crisp, clean air and absorb the majestic views. In his mind, he didn't own the land; he was its steward—a privilege he felt honored to have.

For several minutes, they rode without speaking. Shadows inched over the fields. White-tailed deer crept from a grove of trees. They crested a hill, startling a herd of antelope. The animals sprinted toward a pine-sheltered meadow where he and Bethany had first made love.

His pulse thudded fast at the memory. He'd been nineteen, and so tortured by lust for her that he could barely ride his horse. And when she'd stripped off her clothes amidst the wildflowers, baring her sleek, ripe curves to his gaze…

"That gate's open," she said.

Cole dragged his attention to where she pointed. "You're right." Grateful for the distraction, he tugged on the reins and trotted to the open gate. Bethany joined him a second later, and they both dropped to the ground. He handed her his reins, then strode over and secured the gate.

He paused to study the tire tracks in the grass. "They must have come through here on the way to the stream." Which made sense. They weren't far from a forest service road.

"You have any idea who's doing this?" she asked.

"My father's enemies, I guess."

"Why do you think that?"

"Because ever since he showed up we've been having problems—windows smashed, fences cut." One of his father's mistresses, Gloria Cosgrove, had even attacked him at the bank in town.

Her brows furrowed. "But why? I don't understand the point."

He tipped back his hat and sighed. "I think they're trying to make him leave. Security's tight at the ranch house. My grandmother was a little paranoid and had it rigged like Fort Knox. So if someone wants to hurt him, they need to get him away from the ranch.

"It's no secret that we don't get along." Hell, he despised the man. His father had never kept a promise in his life—not to his wife, not to his children, and certainly not to the gullible constituents who kept voting him into power. "They probably figure if they make my life miserable enough, I'll boot him out."

But unlike the senator, Cole was a man who kept his word. He'd promised to protect his father and he would—no matter what he thought of him.

Bethany hesitated. "You don't think it could be someone else…like one of your men?"

"Why do you ask that?"

She pulled a piece of leather from her pocket and handed it to him. He studied it for a moment, examining the braided horsehair design. "It looks like part of a bridle."

"I found it in your field, not far from the stream. Any idea who it belongs to?"

He shrugged and handed it back. "Tony goes for that kind of thing. Why? You think he's causing the problems?"

"Do you?"

He turned that over in his mind. "No. He's worked for me for a couple of years now. He's reliable." He liked to booze it up on the weekends and brag about his conquests, but there was nothing criminal about that.

Her eyes thoughtful, Bethany stuffed the scrap back into her pocket. "Speaking of your men… I can help with the cattle while I'm here. My father doesn't need me to do much. As long as I check on him occasionally, he'll be fine."

He opened his mouth to agree. But the glint in her eyes brought him up short. He recognized that look—the same stubborn resolve that had made her class valedictorian and earned her a full-ride scholarship to the university back east.

She had an agenda. And if that plan included snooping around and asking questions...

"Forget it," he said. "It's too dangerous."

"I don't see how. And you said you needed more help."

She was right. This was the do-or-die moment for the Bar Lazy K, the only paycheck he'd get all year. Everything hinged on getting those cattle to market—and to do that, he needed help. Even worse, he still had those hundred head stranded in the mountains. If he didn't rescue them before that front moved in, he could lose even more of the herd.

But he refused to put Bethany in danger. And the thought of working beside her made everything inside him rebel. She dredged up too many memories, stirred up longings he'd worked too hard to subdue.

"You know I can do the work," she said.

"That's not the issue." She could run rings around most of his hands.

"Then what is the issue?"

"Whoever's killing my cows is armed. Dangerous." And if she'd come across that shooter in the field... His belly contracted with dread.

"They haven't hurt any people, have they?"

They'd kidnapped his sister. But he couldn't tell her that.

When he didn't answer, she stepped closer. "Listen, Cole, if my dad's in danger, I deserve to know."

"He'll be safe in the house. You both will. I've had the alarm repaired, and there are plenty of people around, including my dad's bodyguards."

"Safe from what?" Exasperation tinged her voice. "Exactly what do you think is going to happen?"

He folded his arms, refusing to say. It wasn't that he didn't trust her—at least in this case. She wasn't the gossipy type. But his father had insisted they keep this mum.

"There's something you aren't saying," she said slowly. "Something else has happened, more than the cows. Something your aunt Bonnie Gene didn't want to say."

He exhaled, knowing he might as well tell her the truth. She was smart. She'd eventually figure it out. And he couldn't take the chance that she'd nose around, asking questions that could get her killed.

He released a sigh. "All right, look. No one outside the family knows this. You have to promise you won't tell anyone, not even your father. I can't let this leak out."

"I promise."

He nodded. "Lana's been kidnapped."

Her face paled. She pressed her hand to her throat. "Kidnapped? When? What happened? *Oh, Cole.*"

"We don't have many details. She's been in Italy, studying art history, getting her master's degree. A few weeks ago she went to Paris on vacation…and disappeared."

He bit down hard on his jaw, suppressing the terror swarming inside him. His sister had to survive. "My dad got a call last week, and she's alive, thank God. But we don't know where she is."

Still looking shaken, Bethany hugged her arms. "What does the FBI say? You've called them, right?"

"My dad has. He has some high-level contacts. All I know is that we're supposed to keep this under wraps."

"What do they want? Money?"

"That's my guess, but they haven't said." More panic ballooned inside him, but he ruthlessly tamped it down. *Lana was fine.* The kidnappers would call and demand the ransom. His father would pay it and bring her home.

"Cole...I'm so sorry." Bethany rested her hand on his arm, her soft, feathery touch a balm to his nerves. "I can only imagine how tough this is. And your poor sister!"

He met her eyes. Her sympathy tugged at something inside him, kicking off a wave of warmth in his chest. Bethany had always understood him. She'd connected with him in a way no one else ever had. They'd been the best of friends, explosive lovers. He'd been so damned crazy in love....

He dropped his gaze to her lips. Time ground to a sudden halt, as if they'd been transported to the past. And any thought of danger flitted away.

She was so close. So beautiful. And the soft, satiny feel of her had burned him alive.

His blood turned heavy and hot. Hunger rose inside him, the need to feel her again in his arms. He widened his stance and shifted closer, his pulse beating fast.

His cell phone chirped. He froze, then straightened, appalled at what he'd been about to do. He couldn't kiss Bethany. He couldn't get anywhere near her. She was the one woman who had the power to make him need her—a risk he couldn't afford.

Determined to keep his mind on track, he whipped out his cell phone and checked the display. The ranch house. He clicked it on with a frown. "Cole here."

"It's your father," his housekeeper, Hannah Brown, blurted out. "You need to come quick."

His heart faltered. "What's wrong?"

"He got a phone call...he looks terrible...all gray... I've phoned the doctor but—"

"I'll be right there." He shoved his phone back into his pocket and launched himself onto the horse.

"What is it?" Bethany swung up onto Red.

"My father." He wheeled the gelding around, then spurred him into a lope. Bethany instantly caught up.

They streaked through the field in silence, taking their mounts to the limit, anxiety pounding his nerves. His father was generally healthy, but the stress of the last few weeks had taken its toll. And if something terrible had happened to Lana…

He cut off that train of thought. His sister had to be all right. He refused to believe the worst.

They reached the county road. Cole leaped down to open the gate.

"Go on," Bethany urged him. "I'll close the gate. Call me if you need help with your dad. Otherwise I'll see you in the morning when we get those cows."

Grimacing at her tenacity, he led his horse through the gate. He didn't want her around. He had enough on his mind with crises erupting at every turn. But nothing mattered more than the ranch.

And as much as it galled him to admit it, he needed help.

"All right." He swung back onto the horse and caught her eye. "You're hired. But you'll stick close to me. You understand? I'm not taking a chance with armed vandals roaming the ranch."

He nudged the horse into a lope, then galloped toward the ranch house, but even the steady drum of hoofbeats couldn't banish his feeling of doom. He would save his ranch. And he'd keep Bethany safe; he'd make damned sure of that.

But could he do the same with his heart?

Chapter 4

Senator Hank Kelley slumped on the sofa in the great room, a clammy sweat moistening his brow, his hands trembling so hard the ice cubes clinked in his highball glass. He knocked back a gulp of Maker's Mark whiskey, feeling the burn scorch straight to his gut.

But even the triple shot of ninety-proof liquor couldn't erase the terror of that call. *They're going to kill Lana. You have to turn yourself in now.*

"You shouldn't drink that. Not until the doctor says it's all right." Hannah, Cole's housekeeper, hovered by the sofa, watching him with the same rabid attention the border collies trained on rebellious cows.

"I told you I'm fine."

"No, you're not. Your face still looks like chalk."

"I had a dizzy spell, that's all." Thanks to the threat he'd just received. The secret society would kill Lana if he didn't surrender; they'd execute *him* if he did.

He took another long swallow of bourbon and shuddered hard. None of this should have happened. Joining the top-secret, ultra-exclusive Raven's Head Society had been his ticket to wealth. He'd felt privileged, powerful, proud.

Until he'd found out they were plotting to assassinate the president of the United States.

He gulped down another slug of whiskey, then wheezed in a shaky breath. He wasn't a murderer, for God's sake. He'd tried to quit the Society, but he knew too much and they refused to let him go. He'd gone to ground, tried to hide, but they'd kidnapped Lana to flush him out.

"Just sit right there," Hannah said. "Don't you dare move. The doctor will be here soon."

He opened his mouth to protest. He was a *senator,* by God. She couldn't order him around. He had a staff to do his bidding, voters clamoring for his attention, beautiful women vying for a turn in his bed.

Senator or not, he'd managed to muck up his life. His doting wife had left him. He'd become a laughingstock in the media, the brunt of late-night comedians' jokes. And instead of fighting back he was hiding out in Montana, cowering behind his bodyguards, while his political enemies attacked him like feral dogs.

And Lana… His stomach went into freefall at the thought of his kidnapped daughter. He'd never dreamed they'd go after her. And where was the mercenary he'd hired? Instead of rescuing her as he was supposed to, the man had gone AWOL for the past two weeks.

Cole's old dog wandered over, then whined and nudged his knee. His lips curling, Hank jerked his leg away. "Get this damned mutt off me. I don't want him slobbering all over my clothes."

Hannah shot him a reproachful look. "Here, Ace. Come on, sweetie. Let's go get you a treat."

The dog turned and trotted off. Annoyed, Hank flicked the fur off his pants. He grabbed the bottle of whiskey from the end table and slopped more into his glass.

The door to the porch burst open. He jumped, his pulse racing off the charts, but Cole strode in, his gaze arrowing straight to him. "What happened?"

Hank gulped down another mouthful of bourbon, hissing as it seared his throat. "Nothing."

"Is it Lana? Did something happen to her?"

"No, nothing happened." *Not yet.*

"Then who called?"

"Nobody. Just Mickey. Mickey O'Donahue."

"The rancher?"

"Yes." O'Donahue owned a ranch near Hank's California estate. He was also a member of the Raven's Head Society, but no one outside the group knew that.

Cole's eyes narrowed, his suspicion clear. "What did he want?"

"Nothing important," Hank fudged. "He just had a suggestion about a business concern."

"And that made you collapse?"

"I didn't collapse. I just got a little dizzy. Hannah overreacted. I told her not to call anyone."

Cole folded his arms, his gaze hard on his father's. Uncomfortable with the scrutiny, Hank mopped the sweat from his brow. The motion made his sore ribs twinge, reminding him of his recent attack in town.

Another frisson of guilt slithered through him. He'd done more than endanger himself and his daughter. He'd brought the Society here to Maple Cove. "I heard about your cows. I…I wish that I could help."

Cole's eyes slitted. Anger vibrated off him in waves.

"I don't need your help. I don't need anything from you at all."

"I know." Cole *didn't* need him. He'd built an impressive business on the family homestead. It wasn't a lifestyle Hank wanted, but it seemed to suit his son. And he'd done it on his own.

An empty feeling spread through his belly, mingling with pride for his son. While he'd been busy working, Cole had grown into a man deserving respect.

"I just…" Hell, this was hard. He wasn't used to apologizing. "I just wanted to say I'm sorry."

"You think that helps?" Hostility rang in Cole's voice. "Your words don't mean a thing. They never have. They aren't going to help Lana, and they're not going to save my ranch." He stomped from the great room into his office, his boots clipping the hardwood floor.

Hank exhaled. Cole was right. He'd been a piss-poor father, making promises he never kept. Not to the voters, not to his children or his wife. It hadn't seemed important. Who had time to attend a kid's birthday party when he had a government to run?

And now… Now it was too late.

He studied the ice cubes melting in his highball glass, aware that he'd screwed up. He'd driven away his family—and someday he'd make amends. But first he had to figure a way out of this mess and bring his daughter home.

But how? He couldn't tell anyone about the Raven's Head Society—not his family, not the police or the FBI.

Not if he wanted to keep his daughter alive.

But if the Society murdered the president…

If anyone got wind that he was involved…

And if that mercenary failed…

"The doctor's here," Hannah announced, hurrying to open the door.

Thoroughly rattled, Hank polished off the bourbon and set aside his glass. And dread burrowed inside him, a chill lodging deep in his gut.

Because he had the terrible feeling events had spiraled beyond his control—and they all would pay the price.

Bethany stood in Red's stall an hour later, still struggling to process Cole's revelation as she brushed the mare. *Kidnapped.* The enormity of it made her reel. She couldn't imagine the terror Lana must be experiencing, the horror of the dreadful ordeal.

She shuddered, wondering how the family was holding up. Lana's mother would be devastated, of course. Cole was obviously furious, especially since his father was at fault.

Was hers?

That thought shot out of nowhere, and she paused with her hand on the horse. No. She refused even to consider it. Her father would never harm an animal, let alone a human being. The idea went against everything she knew of the man.

But if he'd gotten caught in some sort of difficulty, maybe found himself in over his head...

Striving for perspective, she exchanged the currycomb for a softer brush and continued grooming the mare. He was hiding something, she knew that. But it was a huge leap from refusing to answer questions to conspiring to commit a crime. She was letting her imagination run away from her, looking for trouble where it didn't exist.

Still, it was time she demanded answers. She didn't like knowing her father was keeping secrets from her. And if he *was* caught up in something shady, he could be in danger. If the senator's enemies had kidnapped Lana, who knew what else they might do?

She gave Red a final swipe. "All right, time for your grain." Then she needed to talk to her dad.

She set the brush on the corner shelf and moved toward the door of the stall, but a sudden thud reached her ears. She stopped, her heart missing a beat, and whipped her gaze to Red. The mare had her head raised, her ears pricked forward.

The horse had heard it, too.

Her pulse began to race. She stood stock-still, listening intently, hardly daring to breathe. Who was there? Cole? One of the cowboys? But long seconds passed without another sound. She was imagining things. No one was in the barn. The hands were all in the bunkhouse, eating dinner. Besides, Cole had said they were safe near the house.

Chiding herself for her overreaction, she continued to the door. But then another thud came from outside the stall. She froze again, sharp fear blocking her throat. She hadn't imagined that noise. It had come from the direction of the tack room farther down the aisle.

Her hands trembling, she cracked open the door. She peeked out, her throat dust dry, and glanced past the row of stalls. Nothing moved. A horse snuffled from a nearby stall.

Then a cat streaked past in a blur of black, and Bethany pressed her hand to her chest. *The barn cat.* He'd probably knocked something over while hunting—and she'd instantly suspected the worst.

Rolling her eyes at her wild imagination, she went down the aisle to get the grain. She didn't usually jump at shadows. She lived in Chicago, for heaven's sake—and it had a lot more crime than Maple Cove. But learning about Lana's kidnapping had put her nerves on edge.

Still jittery, she scooped out Red's grain and lugged the pail back to the stall. She gave the mare's water a final check, then made herself walk slowly from the barn, refusing to give in to her fears and run.

But she scoured the deepening shadows as she crossed the deserted yard. The pole light blinked on, casting a silvery gleam over the ground, but did little to dispel her nerves. She'd always loved the country at night—the hooting owls, the brilliant canopy of stars, the profound silence gripping the land. But tonight the ranch seemed sinister, empty, exposed.

She glanced at Cole's stone house with its wide, welcoming veranda, and her traitorous thoughts swerved back to him. She didn't want to obsess over Cole. She didn't want to worry about his problems or spend her vacation trying to find out who'd killed his cows.

And she certainly didn't want to think about that moment in the field when she'd thought he was going to kiss her. *Talk about an overreaction!* Her face flamed at the thought. He'd looked at her with those dazzling blue eyes and she'd gone off the deep end, letting her memories sweep her away.

She shook her head in disgust. So Cole still attracted her in a major way. That was hardly a surprise. But she absolutely could not start fantasizing that they had any sort of future. Their relationship had ended. They'd both moved on in their lives.

And she had other problems to worry about—such as discovering why her father had lied.

She found him a few minutes later at the kitchen table, reading the Bozeman paper. "Hi, Dad." Careful of his injuries, she bent down and gave him a hug. "How's your leg?"

"Not bad."

The pallor of his face contradicted that. "You don't look good."

"Don't start hassling me about those pills. I'll take one before I go to sleep."

She sighed at his testy tone. She'd hoped he'd be in a cooperative mood. But maybe a meal would sweeten him up. "What would you like for dinner?"

"I already ate. Hannah brought a tuna casserole by. It's on the counter."

So much for that approach. She went to the sink and washed her hands. "Did Cole call?"

"No. Why would he?"

She exhaled. Lord, he was touchy tonight. "He said the senator wasn't well. I thought he might have needed my help."

"No, no one called."

She dried her hands. "He's probably all right then." Surely they would have heard if the news were bad. She reached up, closed the window above the sink, and caught her father's frown in the glass. "What's wrong?"

He grunted. "What isn't?" He folded his paper and shoved it aside. "That storm front's closing in, and we've got hay to haul, calves to ship to market, cows still stranded in the mountains—and here I sit with this danged bum leg."

She understood his frustration. As foreman, her father should be in the thick of things, directing the work. She scooped some casserole onto a plate, put it in the microwave, and set the time. "So what happened in the mountains?"

Her father leaned back in his chair with a sigh. "A hundred head splintered from the main herd and went up a ravine. I rode in a ways, but they'd disappeared. They've probably holed up in a meadow near the divide. We brought the others back, figuring we'd return in a couple of days to find the rest."

But then he'd broken his leg, and someone had started killing Cole's cows.

She sat in another chair at the table, carefully choosing her words. "Cole wants to start shipping the calves out tomorrow. I told him I'd help."

"I don't want you getting involved."

She blinked, stunned by the vehemence in his voice. "Why not? You don't need me to do anything here—you even said so. And I feel guilty sitting around when Cole's shorthanded. You raised me better than that."

"He can find someone else to help. You stay out of this."

"But why? You have to give me a reason."

He crossed his arms, his mouth set in a stubborn line. "It's not safe."

She leaned her forearms on the table and frowned back, tired of being warned away. She'd grown up around cowboys. She could rope, ride and shoot with the best of them. She could do anything Cole needed on this ranch—drive a truck, deliver calves, castrate and brand a bull. And her father knew that; he'd taught her those skills himself. So what was he afraid of? The men?

"Not safe *how?*" she asked.

When he didn't answer, her exasperation rose. "Come on, Dad. You're not making sense. Cole's shorthanded. He needs help, and he can't find anyone else—not this time of year. And you know I can do the work. So what's really bothering you?"

"Nothing."

"I don't believe you."

"I'm telling you, it's just not safe. Now leave it alone." Still scowling, he tugged his ear.

Her heart plummeted. So he still refused to tell her the truth—but why? What didn't he want her to know?

She tapped her foot, her frustration growing. This

wasn't like her father. If he really did know something, how could he justify not speaking out? What if something happened to the men? How could he live with the guilt?

Tempted to mention Lana, she bit down hard on her lip. Cole had sworn her to silence, and she couldn't betray that trust.

Instead, she pulled the browband she'd found from her pocket and tossed it to her dad. "Any idea who this belongs to? I found it in the field."

His gaze flicked to the leather strap. "No."

"Cole thought it might be Tony's."

He shrugged. "It could be. He has some fancy tack. Hang it in the tack room. Someone will claim it."

Frowning, she picked it up. "So what do you think of Tony? He was a troublemaker in high school."

"He does his work. That's all I care about." His gaze sharpened. "I'm warning you, Bethany. Don't start sniffing around the men, stirring up trouble for Cole. He doesn't need more headaches, especially from you."

She sat back, stung. "What do you mean by that?"

"I'm not blind. I may not talk much, but I can see what's going on. You caused that boy a whole pile of heartache when you left, and he doesn't need you to come back here, meddling in his affairs."

Her jaw went slack. Fierce hurt welled inside. Her father never criticized her. And he'd never questioned her decision to leave.

"He hurt me, too."

He shook his head. "You don't know the half of it. You've got a stubborn streak a mile wide, and when you think you're right, you don't budge."

"I wonder where I got that trait?"

He wagged his finger at her. "I'm warning you. Mind

your own business. That boy doesn't need more grief. Stay out of his affairs."

Rising, he grabbed the crutches propped against the wall. "I'm going to watch TV."

Stunned, she watched him hobble away. The microwave dinged, but she ignored it, her appetite suddenly gone.

She hugged her arms, feeling gutted, trying to figure out what had gone wrong. She'd only wanted answers about the sabotage. Instead her father had attacked her and accused her of hurting Cole.

But he was wrong. Cole had shut *her* out at the end. He'd clammed up, refusing to discuss any options, even to consider leaving the ranch.

And she'd *had* to leave Maple Cove. Her father should have understood that. He knew what people around here were like. Some were all right, like Donald and Bonnie Gene. But there were plenty who had disapproved of her—even threatened her when she'd dated Cole. And she couldn't ignore the insults; she had too much pride.

Her stomach roiling with emotions, she put her plate in the refrigerator and grabbed a jacket, needing air. She went to the front porch and sat on the swing, then stared into the dark. Light from the main house shimmered from the massive windows, spilling out over the lawn.

She'd spent her whole life having proving herself, always having to work harder than anyone else. And by the time she'd graduated from high school, she'd been fed up. She was tired of battling stereotypes, tired of people judging her by her race. She couldn't even enter a store without clerks following her through the aisles, afraid she would steal their goods.

She'd wanted to live where her skin color didn't matter, where people judged her for herself. Where people didn't assume she'd only succeeded because of quotas, or that she hadn't earned her success.

And she'd found that place in Chicago. She had friends, a rewarding job where she could make a difference in people's lives. No one stared at her with suspicion or called her names on the streets.

She sighed, a headache building behind her eyes. She hated to argue with her father. He so rarely lost his temper that it left her shaken and hurt.

And he was dead wrong about Cole.

She rocked the swing, tilted her head back, and closed her eyes. Then, suddenly remembering her patient, Mrs. Bolter—and needing to put something to rights after the debacle with her father—she speed-dialed Adam on her phone.

"Hi, Bethany," he said, picking up.

She sagged back in relief. "Adam. I'm glad I caught you. I've been waiting for your call all day."

"How's Montana? Round up any buffalo?" His words were as light as always, but his joviality sounded forced. Her belly flip-flopped.

Something was wrong.

"No buffalo, just a bunch of ornery cows." She'd fill him in on the danger dogging the ranch when she returned. "So what's going on? Did you find out anything about Mrs. Bolter?" The official report wouldn't come out for weeks, but as lead doctor in the trial, Adam would be the first to know.

"Yeah, but it's not good."

"Not good how?" He didn't answer, and the anxiety in her belly grew. "Come on, Adam. You're making me nervous and I've already had a bad day. What happened?"

The silence stretched. Her forehead began to throb. "Adam? What's going on?"

He cleared his throat. "I probably shouldn't tell you yet, but there was a problem with the dose."

"She overdosed?" Incredulity washed through her. "How? We didn't change anything, and she's been tolerating that level for weeks."

"You're right. It shouldn't have changed. But when we checked the records, it looks like you doubled the dose."

"What?" She sat up straight. "I did not." She scrupulously followed the "five rights" she'd learned in nursing school, reciting them like a mantra every time she administered a drug: *right patient, drug, dose, route, time.* She even checked everything twice. "You know how anal I am about that. There's no way I gave her the wrong dose."

"Hey, I believe you. You don't need to convince me of that. I'm just telling you what they found."

"I'd better come back and clear this up."

"Don't panic. Let me see what I can do first. The investigation has just started."

Her throat closed. "They're investigating me?"

"It's routine, you know that."

"But—"

"Bethany, don't worry. I'll sort this out. I know you wouldn't have made a mistake. That's why I recommended you for the job. Give me a chance to talk to some people and inventory the drug supply, and I'll call you in a couple of days."

Not panic? When the investigators thought she'd made a mistake and caused her patient's death? Adam continued to reassure her, and she ended the call, but she still couldn't catch her breath.

She should fly back tomorrow and defend herself. Her father didn't need her here—and after warning her away from Cole, he'd be happy to see her go. Besides, she'd probably imagined his involvement in the sabotage just as she'd exaggerated that noise in the barn.

But what if she hadn't misjudged him? What if he needed her help?

She pressed her fingers to her forehead, trying to reason this out. Adam could handle the investigation at the clinic. They would check the study-drug supply, see that she hadn't made a mistake. And surely they'd do an autopsy which would further back her up.

Still, she hated being under suspicion. And it felt wrong to sit here idly with her beloved career on the line. She'd worked too hard to let anything derail her now.

She rose, still dithering, when a man emerged from Cole's house. He stood on the porch for a moment, the light shining from the windows silhouetting his powerful build. Gage Prescott, one of the senator's bodyguards. His military bearing gave him away. Then he continued down the steps and disappeared into the night, merging with the shadows like a pro.

She swallowed hard, the feeling of menace she'd experienced in the barn winging back full force. And she knew she couldn't leave. Not yet. Not while danger threatened her father. Not while armed men lurked in the shadows and attacked Cole's ranch.

Shivering, she pulled her jacket's collar closer around her throat. She'd vowed to keep her distance from Cole, sworn she wouldn't get involved. But she couldn't leave here with unanswered questions.

Even if she didn't like what she found.

Chapter 5

"The security system is down again."

Cole took a long swallow of desperately needed coffee, then dragged his attention to his father's bodyguard, Gage Prescott, who stood by the kitchen door. *Great.* Another problem already and the sun had barely come up. "What happened? I thought they just fixed it."

"I don't know, but the entire system is out."

"Any signs of intrusion?"

Gage shook his head. "Not that I could tell."

"So maybe it's just a glitch."

Gage's expression stayed neutral. "Maybe."

Or maybe it was more sabotage. Cole closed his eyes and swore. His ranch had become a war zone.

But it was a war Cole intended to win.

He huffed out a weary sigh. "All right. Call the company, see if they can send someone out right away. They should be open by eight."

He downed the last of the coffee, then glanced out the window at the still-shadowy yard, the thought of someone lurking in the darkness chilling his blood. But Prescott knew what he was doing. He'd keep the senator safe.

And come hell or high water, Cole would protect his ranch.

He strode through the great room, his boots ringing on the hardwood floor. He opened the door for Ace, then paused on the front porch, his breath turning to frost in the air. That front was fast approaching. He had to hurry and get his calves shipped off, then hustle back up to the mountains. If he didn't rescue those cows before the snow set in, he'd lose even more of his herd.

His border collies circling his heels, he crossed the yard to the staging area by the barn. His men stood by their horses and four-wheelers, drinking coffee and warming their hands. No one spoke. None of the usual banter filled the air.

He felt like snarling himself.

He scanned their sullen faces and frowned. "Where is everyone?"

Earl Runningcrane stepped forward. "They rode ahead to get the corrals set up."

"Good." His gaze landed on Bethany. She stood apart from the men, holding Red's reins. She'd donned a vest over her long sleeved T-shirt in deference to the cold. The rising light drew hollows beneath her high cheekbones and dark smudges under her eyes.

His belly tightened, his ingrained response to her beauty ticking him off. He didn't need this distraction. He had enough on his mind without his libido leading him off course.

Determined to rein in the unwanted reaction, he turned to Earl, the seasoned wrangler by his side. "Wait here for the trucks, then direct them to the pasture. Call me on my cell as soon as they show up."

"Right, boss."

Kenny brought over his quarter horse, Gunner. Careful not to look at Bethany, Cole took the reins and leaped astride. "We've got a long day ahead. Let's move out."

"Cole, wait!" He groaned when he heard the shout. His housekeeper ran from the house, waving for him to stop.

"Hold on," he told his men. He clucked to his horse, then rode across the yard, bracing himself for bad news.

Hannah came to a stop. "The trucking company just called. There's a problem with the trucks, a scheduling glitch, and they can't get them here today."

"You're kidding." How the hell had that happened? He'd spent hours on the phone last night making sure it was all arranged. "When can we get them?"

"Tonight, if you can send your own drivers to pick them up. Otherwise you'll have to wait another week."

"A week!" His mood plummeted. No way could he wait that long. He'd lose more cows if he did.

He pinched the bridge of his nose, the dull ache behind his eyes turning into a full-fledged throb. "All right. Tell them I'll send some men up there tonight." He didn't have much choice. But neither could he afford to waste the day.

He wheeled Gunner around and rejoined the men. "Change of plans. We can't get the trucks until tonight, so we're driving the cattle to the barn instead." That would speed up the loading later. But he'd have to dip into his winter hay supply to feed the cows overnight—another unwelcome expense.

Exhaling, he turned to Earl. "Make sure we've got enough hay on hand for tonight. We'll bring them all in except the ones by Rock Creek. They need more time to recoup."

"Got it."

The men began to move out. Cole fell in beside Bethany, a bad feeling swirling inside. Dawn had barely broken, and trouble had already struck twice. He glanced at Bethany astride her horse—her long, black hair shimmering in the rising light, her exotic eyes firing his blood.

And he suspected his problems had just begun.

Bethany trailed the last group of cattle to the barn that afternoon, so tired she could hardly think. Fatigue pounded her skull. Her thighs ached from hours astride the horse. Dust clogged her throat, covering every inch of her with grit.

But even that discomfort couldn't take her mind off Cole.

He loped up the side of the strung-out herd, attracting her attention, just as he had all day. His shoulder muscles rippled beneath his T-shirt. Sweat streaked his dusty jaw. Her gaze lingered on his big hands gripping the reins, the tendons roping his powerful arms, and her body began to hum. Cole was the quintessential cowboy—tough, determined, sexy as all get-out. And there was something about a man doing physical labor that appealed to her in a primitive way.

At least this particular man.

A calf lunged from the herd. Glad for the distraction, Bethany went in pursuit, but the border collie beat her to it and steered it back into line.

"Tony," Cole shouted above the lowing cows. "Get up to the front and start turning them toward the corral." While Tony trotted off, Cole spun around and continued monitoring the herd.

He glanced her way. His amazing blue eyes captured hers, and her heart made a crazy lurch. His strong neck glistened with sweat. Afternoon beard stubble darkened his jaw. And the utter maleness of him rolled through her, inciting a riot of nerves in her chest.

All day long it had been the same—her eyes seeking him out. Their gazes colliding, then skidding away. His incredible sexual appeal winding her tighter than barbed wire on a brand-new fence.

But as he rode off to chase a cow, she had to admit something else. More than his animal magnetism kept drawing her thoughts to him. She couldn't forget her father's accusations, making her wonder if she'd hurt Cole.

And whether it mattered now if she had.

Renewing her resolve to ignore him—and stop obsessing about things she couldn't change—she wiped her forehead on her sleeve and surveyed the herd. They'd worked since dawn, driving hundreds of cows to the corrals by the barn, and now they were nearly done. In a few minutes she could escape into the cabin, take a long, hot bath and *finally* forget about Cole.

Bill swung open the corral gate, and the cows began filing inside. The men watched from their horses and four-wheelers, staying within the cattle's flight zone, but not so close that they'd make them bolt. Bethany glanced at the corral and spotted her father talking with Kenny Greene. He'd hobbled from the cabin on his crutches to watch the calves arrive.

Another calf broke free from the herd, and Bethany nudged Red forward to head it off. Then she swung around, intending to give the calves some space, but Tony rode up, his big gelding crowding her in.

"Back off," she said, fatigue adding an edge to her voice. "You're going to spook the calves."

"The hell I will." His flat eyes narrowed on hers. "I've

been handling cows all my life. I don't need a squaw like you telling me what to do."

She flushed at his favorite insult, but held her ground. "Tell me that when you've scattered the herd."

As if on cue, the cattle behind her panicked. Several lunged for freedom, prompting even more to break from the herd.

Earl Runningcrane trotted up on his quarter horse, dust coating his angry face. "Tony! What the hell are you doing? Give them some space."

Tony glared back. "You're not my boss. I don't take orders from you." But he jerked on the reins and rode off.

"Idiot." Earl turned her way. He asked her something in the Blackfoot language.

Still unsettled, she shook her head. "Sorry. I don't speak Blackfoot."

"Why not?"

"Why should I?"

He studied her for a moment, something that looked a lot like disappointment in his eyes. "No reason." He kicked his horse and went after the fleeing cows.

Exasperated, Bethany turned her attention back to the herd. What was with everyone these days? First her father criticized her decision to leave after high school, now Earl insinuated that she'd ignored her roots.

But why should she speak Blackfoot? She'd never lived on the reservation; she'd grown up in Maple Cove. And so what if she had Indian ancestors? She had Caucasian ones, too.

Still fuming, she trailed the herd to the barn. That was the problem with Maple Cove. Everyone wanted to box her in and label her according to some stereotyped notion they had. No one accepted her for herself.

Especially not Tony. Her belly tightened as he rode past

her and shot her a vicious look. She raised her chin and held his gaze, refusing to back down. He was nothing but a mean-spirited bully who thrived on his victims' fear.

But did that mean he'd killed Cole's cows?

She was still mulling that over as she unsaddled and brushed the mare. She wanted to pin the sabotage on Tony. He'd made her childhood hell, and she'd love to see him pay. But she couldn't prove he'd done anything wrong yet. And aside from his nasty personality, why would he want to hurt Cole?

Unable to come up with an answer, she joined her father at the corral. He leaned heavily on his crutches, his face gray, pain adding more lines around his mouth. "You've been on your feet too long," she scolded. "You'd better get back to the house."

"I guess. The calves look good, though."

She slowed her pace to his, only half listening as he discussed the herd. At least he'd stopped arguing about her helping Cole. But the sight of Earl Runningcrane heading to his truck reminded her of the conversation they'd had.

Not sure how to broach the subject, she waited until her father had finished critiquing the calves. "Say, Dad," she began, feeling awkward. "I was wondering—why didn't we live on the reservation?"

For several minutes he didn't answer. He kept maneuvering his way toward the house, his head bowed, the exertion making him breathe hard. "It would have been too hard on your mother," he finally said.

"In what way?"

"I took her to Browning a couple of times when we first met. My parents didn't accept her any more than her folks accepted me. In the end, it was easier to live in town."

She frowned at that. It hadn't occurred to her that intolerance went both ways. "That couldn't have been easy for you."

"I didn't mind." He stopped when he reached the porch and released a sigh. "I was nearly forty years old when I met your mother. I'd waited all my life to find a woman like her, and when I did… I didn't care where we lived."

"So you sacrificed your happiness for hers."

"Who said I wasn't happy? I just wanted to be with her. And sacrifices come easy when you love someone."

Guilt trickled through her, and she crossed her arms. "It still must have been hard. Living with the prejudice, I mean."

He shrugged. "Sometimes, but people were different back then. And most folks come around if you give them time."

She doubted that. Jerks like Tony never would. And as for the others…she didn't intend to stick around to find out.

Her father hobbled up the porch steps, but his words lingered in her mind. Should she have stayed in Maple Cove? Should she have sacrificed more for Cole? Had she run because she had to—or out of wounded pride?

Feeling uneasy, she cast another look toward the barn. Cole stood outside it, talking to a couple of ranch hands. She studied his steely jaw, the implacable set to his massive shoulders, and slowly expelled a sigh.

No, she'd had to leave. Cole had made his rejection clear. And love went both ways—he could have come with *her* if he'd cared.

But for the first time since she'd left Maple Cove, she couldn't quite banish her doubts.

It didn't help that Cole stopped by that evening to discuss ranch business with her father. Unable to avoid him in the tiny cabin, she retreated to the porch swing while she waited for him to leave. But the deep, sexy timbre of his voice carried in the still night air, further unsettling her nerves.

She still didn't believe she'd hurt him. Her father was wrong about that. But if she *had* made a mistake…

The front door swung open, and he stepped onto the porch. His eyes met hers, and she rose. "Is everything all right?" she asked.

"At the moment." He gripped the back of his neck, and the weary motion tugged at her heart. "But I keep expecting the other shoe to drop."

"I know what you mean. This is the first quiet day since I've arrived." It was almost *too* peaceful. They'd driven the calves to the barn without problems. No one had killed any cows. She glanced into the darkness beyond the yard light, feeling apprehensive at the sudden lull.

"I'm going to check on the calves by the barn." He angled his head to meet her eyes. "You want to come?"

Her heart stumbled. Warnings went off in her mind. She should decline. A walk in the moonlight was too cozy, too seductive, *too intimate*.

But she'd never been able to resist Cole.

"Sure," she heard herself say.

She followed him down the porch steps, wondering if she'd lost her mind. She should be avoiding Cole, not strolling with him beneath the stars.

Shaking her head at her lapse in judgment, she stuffed her hands in her jacket pockets to keep them warm. "Where is everyone? The ranch seems deserted tonight."

"I sent four men to Butte to get the stock trucks. The rest are on patrol." His gaze swiveled to hers, and the impact ripped through her, rattling her pulse. "I wanted to let you know that the security system is down. They'll fix it tomorrow when the part comes in, and I've stepped up patrols around the house. But I thought you should know."

She flicked her gaze from the shadows surrounding the barn to the profound darkness cloaking the fields, and a chill scuttled down her spine. Someone was out there, watching their movements. Someone wanting to do them harm.

Suddenly the barn cat flitted past, making her heart race even more. Should she mention the thuds she'd heard in the barn to Cole? But what would be the point? He had enough on his mind without her wild imaginings adding to his stress.

But with the security system down...

Still uncertain, she walked beside him around the barn, her feet crunching on the gravel path. The cold wind gusted, and she zipped up her jacket against the chill.

"Are you cold?" Cole asked.

"Not too bad."

His gaze ran over her face, a crease forming between his dark brows. "Something's bothering you, though. You've looked preoccupied all day."

Surprised he'd noticed, she stopped beside the corral and propped her forearms on the fence. She didn't want to discuss their breakup—at least not yet. Not until she had a better handle on exactly what had gone wrong. And she couldn't mention her suspicions about Tony since she had nothing to base them on.

"I've just had some problems at work, that's all," she finally said.

"What kind of problems?"

She studied his eyes, tempted to tell him. Standing together like this, cocooned in the quiet darkness, it was easy to forget the heartbreak and remember the camaraderie they'd shared.

And he'd revealed his sister's kidnapping to her.

"I work at a research clinic," she said. "The Preston Werner Clinic in Chicago. We've been conducting a trial for an experimental rheumatoid arthritis drug called Rheumectatan. The night before I came here, one of my patients died."

"That's tough."

"It gets worse." She pressed her hand to her belly to settle her nerves. "They think I administered the wrong dose, that I made a mistake that caused her death."

"You'd never do that."

She looked at him in surprise.

He shrugged. "You're too careful. I spent enough time studying with you to know that."

They hadn't always studied.

Awareness arced between them. Sudden heat flared in his eyes. And she knew he was remembering the same thing she was—the hours they'd spent in erotic exploration, touching, kissing, making love…

Her pulse scrambling, she jerked her gaze back to the cows. The past was gone. She was not going to dwell on their sex life or how madly in love she'd been.

Struggling to gather her composure, she cleared her throat. "Thanks. I appreciate the vote of confidence."

"It's a fact. You're the most conscientious person I know."

She braved another glance his way. Light spilled from the barn, dusting him with a silver sheen, highlighting the hard, male planes of his face. Their eyes locked again, and something else shimmered between them, something beyond the lust—a feeling of friendship, warmth, *trust*.

But hadn't that been an illusion? Hadn't he callously shut her out?

He propped his boot on the fence and looked away, breaking the spell. "So what do you think happened?"

She dragged in a breath, trying to marshal her scattered thoughts. "I don't know. Maybe the drug caused a bad reaction or interacted with an underlying condition she had. But Adam would have screened her for that. He's the doctor running the trial."

Cole's gaze traveled back to hers. "Can you check her records?"

"Yes." She knew the password and could access the system online. "But I doubt I'll have to. When they inventory the study drug, they'll notice the discrepancy and see that they made a mistake.

"By the way," she added. "I haven't mentioned this to my father. I don't want him to worry." Or think she'd failed at her job. "I'd appreciate it if you keep this quiet for now."

"Sure." Cole turned his gaze to the cows, his expression thoughtful. The calves shuffled and lowed in the pens. A moment later, he straightened, and they started back toward the house.

"Tell me more about your life in Chicago," he said.

She nodded, grateful for the change of subject. "Well, I love my job. And I've got a great apartment near the lake. No view to speak of." Nothing like the stunning mountain vistas on his ranch. "But I'm close to all the action, so there's always a lot to do."

But somehow, walking beside Cole in the moonlight with millions of stars glittering above her, Chicago didn't seem that great.

"So you like it?" he asked.

"Yes." Of course she did. "It's just what I'd hoped it would be."

"I'm glad." They stopped at the steps to her porch. His eyes stayed on hers, and time seemed to disappear. How many nights had they spent like this—walking in the moonlight, gazing into each other's eyes?

The moment stretched. She knew she should step back, climb up the steps and say good-night. But emotions tumbled inside her—longing, regret.

Desire.

His eyes narrowed. Heat radiated from his muscled build. And his raw masculinity rolled through her, making her heart rate spike.

And suddenly, she wanted desperately to feel him, to stroke her palms down his stubbled jaw, to feel his hard, warm lips devouring hers.

He wanted to kiss her, too. She couldn't mistake the hunger in his eyes this time.

But that was insane. Nothing good could come from a kiss. They had too much baggage between them, and they couldn't change the past.

Cole reached down, tucked a loose strand of hair behind her ear, and her heart began to thud. Then he cupped her jaw with his work-roughened hand, sending thrills rushing over her skin.

"Cole…" she whispered, but whether as a plea or a warning, she didn't know.

His gaze dropped to her mouth. Her heart tried to burst from her chest. And a fierce sense of yearning mushroomed inside her, the need to lose herself in the strong, solid feel of him making her sway.

Then he dipped his head, and his lips took hers—hard and potent and warm, sending a hot blast of need sizzling and skipping through her veins. She gripped his rock-hard arms, her knees suddenly buckling, a moan forming deep in her throat.

She'd missed this. *Missed him.* Nothing had ever felt so right.

But, way too soon, he ended the kiss. He stared down at her for a moment, their ragged breaths dueling in the night. Then he stepped back and cleared his throat.

"I'm glad you found what you were looking for," he rasped. He turned on his heel and strode away.

Her heart pounding, her entire body trembling, she grabbed the porch rail for support and watched him go.

He reached his house, paused to pet Ace waiting beside the steps. Then he bent down, gently picked up the arthritic dog, and carried him inside.

And, as a deep hush settled around her, Bethany couldn't help but wonder—if she'd found everything she'd wanted in Chicago, why did she feel bereft?

Cole didn't often have regrets, but that kiss ranked up there as one of the biggest mistakes he'd ever made.

He sprawled in his bed hours later, his sheets tangled and sweaty, so wound up he couldn't sleep. What in the hell had he been thinking? He'd spent the entire day trying to avoid her, only to blow it at the end.

He'd had no business walking with her in the darkness, no business asking about her life. He should have told her about the broken security system on the porch, then marched straight back to his house. But she'd looked so damned beautiful standing there in the moonlight, like every fantasy he'd ever had.

He punched his pillow and sighed, knowing that more than her looks had caused him to cave. Her beauty he could have resisted, although everything about her still turned him on. It was that sense of connection, that *rightness* she'd made him feel that had caused him to lose his mind.

So he'd messed up and succumbed to a moment of weakness. Somehow he had to forget it and make sure he didn't do it again. There was no point torturing himself with needs he couldn't indulge.

He rubbed his scratchy eyes, glanced at the clock beside his bed, and groaned. Two o'clock. If he didn't get some shut-eye soon, he'd never make it through the day.

Hoping a drink would take the edge off, he rolled out of bed, and pulled on his shirt and jeans. Then he strode down the hall toward the great room, detouring to the wet bar off to the side. Ace padded toward him and whined, and Cole reached down to scratch his ears. "Hey, buddy. You having trouble sleeping, too?"

Still whining, Ace turned and trotted toward the door.

"All right, give me a minute and I'll let you out." He opened the bar, pulled out a bottle of Scotch and splashed some into a glass. Then he knocked it back, hoping the fiery drink would deaden the lust.

The dog yipped and pawed at the door. "All right. I'm on my way. You don't need to wake everyone up." He poured more Scotch into the tumbler, then stuck the bottle back into the bar. His glass in hand, he headed toward the front door.

A glow in the windows caught his eye. His heart stopped, a sudden feeling of wrongness surging inside. He slammed down his glass on a nearby table, bolted to the door, and flung it open.

The barn was engulfed in flames.

Chapter 6

Cole gaped at the bright orange flames leaping across the barn in the darkness, twisting and curling like macabre dancers into the sky. Horses screamed from inside the burning building. The fierce fire crackled and roared. Cole launched himself back into the great room in a burst of adrenaline, then sprinted full out down the hall.

Veering into the guest wing, he whipped his cell phone from his pocket and pounded on his father's door. He needed to alert his ranch hands. He had to get those horses out fast. It would take the volunteer fire department half an hour or more to get here, and he couldn't afford to wait.

Speed-dialing the bunkhouse, he hammered again on the door. The noise drew Bart, the bodyguard on the night shift, from the adjacent lounge.

"The barn's on fire," Cole barked into the phone, but he kept his gaze on Bart. "Get everyone on it. And call the fire department in Maple Cove."

Comprehension crossed Bart's face. His father's other bodyguard, Gage Prescott, raced from his bedroom with his weapon drawn, just as the senator flung open his door.

"Take the senator and Hannah into the safe room," Bart told Gage, referring to the wine cellar, the most secure spot in the house. "I'll scout around outside."

Gage nodded, his eyes grim. "Be careful. It could be a trap, an attempt to lure the senator outside."

Cole's belly tightened. Trap or not, he had to fight the fire.

Leaving the bodyguards to deal with his father, he raced into the mudroom and jerked on his boots. Then he hurtled out the back door and sprinted flat out toward the barn, desperate to save the animals inside.

Heavy smoke rolled from the roof now. Vivid orange flames spiraled upward, sending sparks shooting into the sky. His eyes watered and stung as he neared the barn, and he coughed on the acrid smoke. He had to free the horses, then try to move the calves. They were in the worst possible place, penned in the corral behind the barn.

He charged toward the barn, his breathing ragged. Someone darted ahead of him through the billowing smoke. *Bethany.* His heart stopped when she ran inside.

"Bethany!" he shouted, but she didn't hear.

Swearing, his throat tight with fear for her safety, he plunged after her into the barn. Burning wood rained from the rafters. The roar of the fire filled the air. He coughed, his eyes stinging from the heavy smoke, searching frantically to see where she'd gone.

He spotted her ahead of him, flinging open Red's stall. "Go on! Get out!" she yelled at the horse, who was prancing and neighing with fear.

The crazed horse burst from the stall. Cole flattened

himself to the wall as the mare thundered past, her eyes wild with terror as she fled the barn.

Flames crackled and hissed around them. Dense smoke hung in the air. Cole launched himself into action, lunging from stall to stall, helping Bethany throw open the doors. Several horses instantly bolted to safety, but the rest refused to budge.

He suddenly lost sight of Bethany, and panic slammed through his nerves. But the smoke shifted, then parted, and Bethany appeared, towing another horse toward the door. A beam fell nearby, and the thoroughbred started trotting in tight circles, his ears flat to his head.

"Stay outside! I'll get the rest," he shouted to her as she hurried past, battling to control the terrified horse.

With no time to waste, Cole darted into the nearest stall. Tony's roan gelding reared up, his eyes rolling back as sparks sizzled and popped nearby. Cole tried to throw on his halter, but the gelding pawed and tossed his head.

"Come on, damn it! I'm trying to save your life!" Coughing, his eyes streaming from the pungent smoke, Cole lunged again at the horse. He managed to toss on his halter, then hauled the skittish horse from the stall. They burst from the barn, the gelding rearing and kicking, and Cole let go of the lead. The horse raced into the night.

Cole wiped his eyes, then straightened and hauled air to his searing lungs. Men now shouted and ran around him, using shovels and hoses to fight the fire. He glimpsed Rusty through the smoke, balancing on his crutches, hosing down the cabin to keep the sparks from igniting the roof. Others leaped aboard tractors and balers, rushing to get the machinery out of harm's way.

Earl Runningcrane dashed over, his face covered with soot. "Boss! I opened the gates and let the cattle out. They were starting to stampede."

"Good." Cole was grateful he'd thought to check. "Take charge of the men. I'll get the rest of the horses out."

Bethany darted past him, then ran back into the barn, and his belly went rigid with fear. The fire was mounting, pushing sparks over the yard, threatening to explode. He had to get her back out!

Swearing, he ducked into the barn behind her, choking in the roiling smoke. The air had become a furnace, and sweat streamed down his face and back. Horses whinnied above the roar. His heart banged against his chest. Bethany came from a stall with a thrashing horse, determination etched on her face.

"Wait outside," he shouted, hoping she listened this time. "I'll get the final two."

He hurried into Gunner's stall, then circled behind him, trying to force the horse to move. But Gunner balked and kicked, narrowly missing Cole's chest.

"Come on, come on!" he urged. Knowing every second counted, he grabbed the halter and flung it over Gunner's head. Then he hauled the panicked horse from the stall and got him moving toward the open door.

But a section of roof crashed nearby, flinging up ashes and sparks. Gunner reared up, threatening to strike him with his flailing hooves. Cole gritted his teeth, using all his strength to pull him from the burning barn.

He let go of the horse and turned back, heaving air to his fiery lungs. He coughed, gagging on the pungent smoke, but couldn't take time to rest. He had one more horse to get out.

But the fire was growing stronger, more volatile, fanned by the gusting wind. Embers shot from the roof, torching spot fires. Flames roared with deadly menace, the barn on the verge of collapse.

Bethany dashed back inside. Cole's heart halted, stark

fear strangling his throat. She'd never make it. The rest of the roof was about to collapse!

Terrified, he went in pursuit. Flames crackled around him. The tack room had become a raging wall of fire. Dodging falling timbers, he sprinted toward the remaining stall.

The air vibrated as the fire gained fury. Black smoke streamed from the flames.

And a wild feeling of panic churned inside him. No horse was worth Bethany's life.

"Bethany!" he hollered, but he couldn't see her through the stinging smoke. His urgency at a flash point, he vaulted a burning log, then plowed through the wall of heat. Flames hissed and crackled on every side.

Then Bethany appeared with Bill's horse, Blaze, her eyes wild in her blackened face. She'd thrown a halter on the horse, and had a towel draped over his head.

The flames grew more erratic. The fire boiled up behind them, roaring like a freight train in the trembling air.

They only had seconds left.

He grabbed the lead from her hands. "Go!" he shouted, relieved when she listened and ran toward the door.

Another beam broke free and fell. Blaze reared, and Cole battled to hang on to the lead. His pulse rocketing, his muscles straining, he pulled the frenzied horse outside.

A deafening boom came from behind him. Men shouted and sprang away. Cole released the horse, then whipped around as the roof of the barn collapsed.

Sparks shot over the yard. Coughing and wheezing badly, Cole hauled air into his scorched lungs. They'd made it. They'd gotten out safely.

But Bethany had nearly died.

Desperate to find her, he searched through the chaos in the yard. He spotted her off to the side, bent over double, her hands braced on her knees. Swamped with relief, he closed his eyes and struggled to control his rioting nerves. But he couldn't calm down, couldn't contain the emotions careening inside. He could have lost her inside that barn.

Urgently needing to touch her, he strode across the yard. She straightened, and their eyes connected through the drifting smoke. He caught the telltale wobble of her mouth, the vulnerable sheen in her eyes and suddenly lost control.

He reached her and grabbed her arms. "What the hell were you thinking? How could you risk your life like that?"

Her full lips parted. Her eyes turned huge in her face. "I had to save the horses. I couldn't let them die."

So she'd risked her life instead.

Men sprinted around them. His lungs heaving, Cole grappled to regain control. He didn't want to care about her. He didn't want to feel these emotions bulging inside. He tightened his hold on her slender arms, the fragile feel of her making him angrier yet.

She bit her lip, her eyes uncertain in her sooty face. Shudders wracked her slender body—shock from the near-death experience setting in.

Swearing, he pulled her close and enveloped her in his arms. Then he closed his eyes, absorbing the tremors running through her, inhaling the smoky smell of her hair. And despite his fury, despite his terror that she could have died, he couldn't help but admire her courage in entering that barn.

Firebrands dropped around them. Embers sailed past in the wind. A hot spot took off beside them as the fire made a run across the dried grass.

"Watch out, boss!" someone shouted.

Jolted back to reality, Cole pulled Bethany to safety farther away from the barn. Then, not trusting himself around her, he forced himself to let her go and step back.

But his gaze continued to devour her, sweeping the delicate line of her jaw, the ashes clinging to her unbound hair, the vulnerable curve of her lips.

"I...I'd better go help my dad," she whispered, her voice raspy from breathing smoke.

Too overcome to speak, he didn't answer. She turned, and he watched her go, shaken to the core by the feelings she'd evoked. Like ripping a bandage from a wound, she'd bared feelings he'd kept buried for years, leaving him vulnerable, raw, exposed.

And no way could he let that happen. He couldn't care. He couldn't let himself like her again. Because caring would lead to heartbreak when she left.

And he refused to give her the power to destroy him again.

Gathering his scattered defenses, he turned to face his barn. All that remained was a heap of burning rubble— a bonfire blazing in the night. His men stood motionless beside it, knowing nothing would save it now.

Suddenly depleted, he watched the bright flames twirl against the sky. Everything he'd worked for—the safe, reliable world he'd built—had just gone up in smoke.

And he feared that nothing would ever be the same.

Several hours later, as dawn broke against the eastern sky, Cole once again stood by his barn. Exhaustion hammered his skull. The acrid stench of burnt wood stung his sinuses, filling the air with a murky haze. He took a pull from a bottle of water, the extent of the destruction making him numb.

The barn was toast. The pumper truck from Maple Cove's volunteer fire department continued to douse the water on smoldering logs, but there was nothing left to save.

He rubbed his stinging eyes and exhaled, struggling to make sense of the fire. He doubted an electrical problem had caused it; he'd upgraded the wiring when he'd renovated the barn. He'd also installed a state-of-the-art sprinkler system—which had failed to come on.

He hardened his jaw, unable to avoid the conclusion that had been dancing on the periphery of his mind all night. The fire had to be arson. Anything else was too coincidental, given the recent attacks on his ranch.

One of the volunteer firefighters walked over, drawing Cole's gaze. "The fire inspector is on his way," he said. "I'm sending the trucks back now. We'll keep one here in case there are any flare-ups."

Cole nodded. "Thanks, Bob. I appreciate the help." Although it wouldn't do any good.

Grimacing, he returned his gaze to the rubble. His cows were scattered across the fields, his horses traumatized from the ordeal. He could only thank God that none of his ranch hands had been hurt.

His thoughts veered back to Bethany and that nerve shattering moment when she'd entered the collapsing barn. He shuddered, not wanting to remember the terrifying ordeal. Because the thought of her risking her life…

He quickly blocked off the thought. She'd survived. *She was fine.*

But he knew one thing. He had to keep his distance. He couldn't let down his guard. There'd be no more intimate talks. No more moonlit walks. And he definitely wouldn't kiss her again. He would stay far away from Bethany until her vacation was up and she returned to Chicago where she belonged.

Earl Runningcrane jogged up, his hair wet from a recent shower. "Hey, boss. Just to let you know, we've rounded up the horses. They're in the pasture behind the house."

Cole ran his hand through his filthy hair, dislodging ashes and soot. "Any injuries?"

"Not that I could tell. We'll check them better once the trucks leave and the commotion dies down. They're too nervous to let us close." He paused. "How are the cows?"

Cole exhaled. "Several got injured in the stampede. The vet's on his way." He hoped they didn't have to put them down. It would be his own damned fault if they did. If he'd left them to graze in the fields, if he hadn't insisted on saving a few hours of work by penning them close to the barn....

"The fire inspector's on his way, too," he added.

"I'll wait for them if you want to get some breakfast," Earl offered. "I already ate."

Cole nodded, suddenly aware of his gnawing hunger. "I won't be long. I'll grab a shower and something to eat. Call me as soon as they show up."

His steps weary, he trudged toward the house. He skirted the porch, then veered toward the mudroom around the back, knowing Hannah would skin him alive if he went traipsing through the great room covered in soot.

He inhaled, his chest still fiery from breathing smoke. He didn't need the inspector to tell him the fire was arson. He had no doubts about that. What he didn't know was whether one of his ranch hands was to blame.

A sick feeling broke loose inside him at the thought. He knew his men. He'd worked beside them for years. He'd even attended high school with some and played on the same sports teams. And they'd never given him a reason to doubt their loyalty.

But he couldn't ignore the facts. Whoever had torched his barn had known that he was shorthanded. He'd known that Cole had sent men off last night to get those cattle trucks. And he'd managed to set the fire, disabling the security system and sprinklers, without anyone noticing him hanging around—or tipping off the dogs.

Cole tightened his jaw, the idea that he had a traitor in his midst was a kick to the throat. He didn't tolerate betrayal.

And anyone who abused his trust would pay the price.

He neared the mudroom door and glanced up, then spotted a mound of clothes on the stoop. No, not clothes, something covered by a blanket. He slowed to a stop and frowned. That hadn't been there when he'd left the house.

Sudden trepidation gripped him. He scanned the bumpy mound, his heart beginning to thud. Then he spotted something peeking out from beneath the blanket.

A human hand.

His lungs closed up. His blood coursed hard in his skull. He skirted the pile and made out a pair of boots. Military boots, he realized with a jolt, belonging to a man wearing camouflage clothes.

His heart slamming against his rib cage, he whipped back around and scanned the yard. The horses still stood in the field beyond the windbreak. The branches of the cottonwoods swayed, their leaves fluttering in the morning breeze. The muted roar of the pumper truck droned from near the barn.

Nothing else moved. Nothing seemed out of place.

But someone had dumped a corpse.

Dread trickling through him, Cole turned back to the man. He made himself approach him, then tugged off the blanket and nudged him over with his foot.

He was definitely dead—executed, judging by the bullet hole between his eyes.

Swallowing a spurt of bile, Cole forced himself to study the bloodless face. He had dark, military-style hair, a neatly trimmed goatee. He appeared to be in his thirties, medium height with a muscular build.

Cole knew one thing. He'd never seen him before.

So what was a dead soldier doing here?

Cole pulled out his cell phone and punched in a number.

"Prescott," his father's bodyguard answered.

"We've got a problem. There's a dead body at the mud-room door."

"I'll be right there."

Cole clicked off the phone and slid it into the pocket of his jeans. He continued circling the man, then spotted an envelope tucked into his belt.

He stepped closer. The envelope was addressed to *him*.

His pulse accelerating, he crouched down, tugged a bandana from his pocket so he wouldn't erase any finger-prints, then carefully extracted the envelope from the sol-dier's belt.

Still using the bandana, he opened it, pulled out a type-written note, and read the words:

Turn the senator over now—or the Indian woman will die.

Chapter 7

Cole stood beside his father's bodyguards and stared at the murdered man, feeling as though he'd crash-landed in an alien world. The kidnappers had done far worse than burn his barn or shoot his livestock. They'd executed this unknown man.

Stark fear trickled through him. A terrible sense of foreboding whispered up his spine. These same murderers were holding his sister hostage. They'd invaded his property and dropped off a corpse on his doorstep—proving how close they could get.

And they'd threatened to kill Bethany next.

The muscles of his belly tightened. He shifted his gaze to the wide-open fields surrounding his ranch, feeling like a lab rat trapped in a maze. Exactly who was he fighting? Where were they watching him from? And why had they killed this man?

His thoughts swerved to his father, and he curled his

hands into fists. His father *had* to know more than he'd let on.

And it was time he revealed the truth.

His anger stirring, Cole turned toward the mudroom. But the door swung open, and his father stepped outside. "What's going on here?" he boomed with his usual bluster.

His gaze dropped to the man lying motionless on the stoop, and the blood drained from his face. "Oh, God. He…he's dead." He swayed, then clutched the porch post for support.

Cole lunged forward and grabbed his arm. "Are you all right?"

The senator's dazed eyes met his, the fading bruises standing out on his ashen face. "No, of course I'm not all right. He's dead!"

Cole went still. "You know this man?"

"Yes." The senator turned even grayer, then flicked an uneasy glance at the corpse. "He's Rick Garrison. I hired him to rescue Lana."

"Oh, hell," Gage Prescott said, his voice thick with disgust.

"He is—*was*—a mercenary. Former Special Forces. He was supposed to be one of the best."

And the kidnappers had managed to kill him. Cole's veins filled with ice.

"I hired him two weeks ago," his father continued. "I had to do something. I was desperate. I was afraid they were going to hurt Lana. But we lost contact. He didn't call or check in with me like we'd arranged." More color leached from his face. "Now I know why."

Cole dragged his gaze back to the dead man. The hair stirred on the nape of his neck. His father's enemies had taken out a professional sniper.

Who the hell were they up against?

"Who killed him?" he asked.

His father didn't answer, and Cole's hold on his patience slipped. "Damn it, I need to know! These people have kidnapped Lana. They've shot my cows, burned my barn and now they've murdered this man. I need to know what's going on before anyone else gets killed."

He thrust the note at his father, fury vibrating his voice. *"No. More. Lies."*

"He's right," Gage said. "You need to come clean. And it's time we involved the police."

His father unfolded the note and read it. Then he sagged against the support beam, his face so ashen Cole leaped forward again to help.

His father waved him off. "You're right. I…I'll tell you. All of you. Everything." He dragged in a reedy breath. "You'd better call the sheriff and get him out here. Call Donald and Bonnie Gene. And Dylan…put him on the speaker phone."

His face bloodless, he shuddered hard. "I…I'll be waiting inside." He handed the note to his bodyguard, then stumbled into the house.

Still furious, Cole swung his gaze back to the murdered man. He intended to get answers, all right. His father wasn't evading his questions this time. Because more than his cattle ranch was now at stake.

They were fighting for their lives.

Hank Kelley slumped on the sofa in the great room an hour later, staring at the whiskey in his highball glass. *Liquid courage.* He needed it today. The moment he'd dreaded for weeks had arrived. He had to reveal what a fool he'd been.

He lifted his gaze to his half brother, Donald, sitting

across from him in a chair, his wife, Bonnie Gene, at his side. Donald had barely spoken to him since he'd arrived, his disdain for him clear. And when he learned what else Hank had done…

He gulped down another swallow of whiskey as the rest of the group took their seats—the county sheriff, Wes Colton, was there, as well as the ranch foreman, Rusty, and his daughter, Bethany, who'd received the threat in the note. Cole stood between the two bodyguards, his arms crossed, his face as unyielding as the rocks on the fireplace along the wall.

He was about to get angrier yet.

"More drinks, anyone?" Hannah asked, her white hair sticking up in clumps after the harrowing night.

Cole shook his head. "We're fine, Hannah, thanks." He trained his gaze on Hank. "Let's get this started."

Hank nodded, his stomach a jumble of nerves. He downed the last of his whiskey and set the glass aside. Clasping his hands, he glanced at the laptop Cole had propped on the coffee table so his son in California could listen in.

"I, um…" He cleared his throat and tried again. "I told you that my political enemies were after me, causing these problems. But that's…not exactly right."

Unable to face their censure, he dropped his gaze to his hands. "A few months ago, I got an invitation to join a private society, very exclusive. Secretive, actually." He let out a nervous hum. "The members keep a really low profile. They work behind the scenes, influencing the banks, world markets. Real movers and shakers." The kind that never made the news. "I thought they'd advise me about investments, increase my wealth…."

In truth, he'd been inflated with self-importance, convinced he'd made it to the big leagues, that he was one of the elite.

"Does this society have a name?" Sheriff Colton asked, taking notes.

Hank pressed his slick palms to his thighs. "It's called the Raven's Head Society." He flushed, realizing how ridiculous it sounded now.

But there was nothing ridiculous about their plans.

"They, um...aren't just involved in financial matters. They get involved in politics, too."

All eyes stayed on him. The clock on the mantel ticked. He sucked in a breath, fierce shame heating his face. He'd give anything not to have to admit this, but Rick Garrison's death had forced his hand.

"It turns out they have a plan. I didn't know about it or I'd never have gotten involved."

The sheriff's eyes sharpened. "What kind of plan?"

Hank closed his eyes. "They're plotting to assassinate the president."

Hannah gasped. A shocked hush fell over the group.

"President Colton?" Cole asked a moment later, his voice ringing with disbelief.

"Yes." Hank gave the sheriff an apologetic shrug. The sheriff and the president were distant relations. And two of the sheriff's brothers had married Donald's daughters, linking his family to the president, too. "I swear I didn't know. As soon as I found out their plans, I quit. Or at least I tried to."

Hank braved a glance at his brother. Donald's eyes reflected his disgust—which Hank knew he deserved. "I really did try to quit," he repeated. "But I knew too much and they wouldn't let me go."

"I hope to hell you notified the president about this," Cole said.

"I couldn't. These people have too much power," Hank said when Cole opened his mouth to argue. "You have no idea. They've got ties everywhere—even to the president. I couldn't trust anyone with the truth, including the police."

He cringed. "The society wanted me to turn myself in to them. But they'd kill me if I did. They can't take the chance that I'll talk. That's why they took Lana, to force me out of hiding. So I hired that mercenary, hoping he could get her free."

Instead, Hank had signed the death warrant of an innocent man.

For a moment no one spoke. Looking grim, the sheriff continued to jot down his notes. Hank picked up his highball glass, realized it was empty, and set it back down.

"Wait a minute," Cole said slowly. "You said you couldn't trust anyone, not even the police. Then who did you contact in the FBI?"

Hank swallowed hard. This was the worst part, what he hated most to admit. "I never called them."

"What?" Cole exploded. "These murderers are holding Lana hostage and threatening to kill the president, and you didn't tell the FBI?"

"I couldn't. I knew they'd kill her if I did. And I thought I could handle this on my own."

"The hell you did." Cole's voice trembled with outrage. "You wanted to protect yourself and your damned career."

He was right. Hank's shoulders sagged. "My career would have been over if word of this got out."

Cole hissed. "You've been lying all this time. Lana's life's at stake and all you can think about is your job."

"I never wanted her to get hurt. I didn't know they'd go after her. And when they did... I thought Garrison would rescue her, that he would bring her home before anyone else found out. He was supposed to be the best."

He dropped his gaze to the floor. He knew he deserved

their disgust. Even he was appalled by the depths to which he'd sunk.

The sheriff put away his notepad and pulled out his cell phone. "I'm contacting the FBI. They can notify the president's detail and anyone else who needs to know." His voice turned hard. "They'll need to question you. We can do it here or at the station, your choice. But from now on you're going to cooperate fully on this."

Hank nodded, knowing he had no choice. He couldn't deal with this alone anymore. Rick Garrison's murder had proven that.

"Let us know what we can do," Cole told the sheriff, his voice gruff. "We've got to get Lana back."

"That poor girl," Bonnie Gene whispered, and her husband pulled her close.

Hank stole a glance at the group. The ranch foreman and his daughter had their heads together. Cole had walked over to comfort Hannah, who stood by the kitchen, clutching her cat in her weathered hands. Even the bodyguards had tuned him out.

He experienced a sudden pang. He was the odd man out here, the one who didn't belong. He'd screwed up so many times that his family had rejected him. Sure, Cole had taken him in when he'd needed help—but he'd done it out of duty, not love.

A heavy feeling unfolded inside him, but he knew he only had himself to blame. He'd taken his family for granted, not realizing that love came from respect—which he had failed to earn.

"I'm going to fix this," he said.

Cole scoffed. "Cut the bull. No one believes a damned thing you say anymore."

"Cole," Bonnie Gene warned, her voice sharp. "That's no way to speak to your father."

"No, he's right," Hank admitted. "I haven't given him— any of you—a reason to believe me before." But that was about to change. He was going to earn back their respect and trust.

But *how?*

He frowned, his mind running through options. He'd put Lana in jeopardy, so he had to get her out. But he needed a plan—one he carried out himself this time. That mercenary had sacrificed his life for a woman he didn't know. How could Hank do less for his own flesh and blood?

The meeting began to break up, but he sat motionless in his seat. For once he couldn't spin his way out of this mess, couldn't blame it on someone else. He had to man up, take responsibility for his mistakes, and put his life on the line to save his daughter from certain death.

But did he have the nerve?

Bethany sat immobile, the enormity of the senator's revelation robbing her of breath. A sinister society had captured Lana. They were plotting to kill the president of the United States. Now they'd murdered a man and dumped his body on Cole's back doorstep—bringing the violence even closer to them.

She shuddered, unable to believe it. This seemed like something from a Hollywood thriller, not part of her real life.

And it was all the senator's fault.

She shot a glance at Cole's father, the depth of his self-absorption boggling her mind. How any man could sacrifice his family to his career… She shook her head. And maybe he hadn't set out to endanger Lana, but his daughter had paid the price.

So had Cole.

She skipped her gaze across the great room. Cole stood

near the windows talking on his cell phone, the weary slump of his shoulders tugging at her heart. She'd known Cole and his father weren't close, that the senator had ignored his children growing up, but she'd never realized the extent of his neglect. Proof of his calloused behavior came as a shock.

And, like it or not, it also forced her to rethink the past.

She handed her father his crutches, then rose. She didn't want to dredge up those memories. The past was gone. There was no point dwelling on things she couldn't change.

But her mind kept flashing back to the day she and Cole had broken up. She'd found out about her scholarship. She'd rushed to tell him the news. She'd expected him to be pleased, proud of what she'd accomplished after so many years of hard work. Instead, he'd closed down. He'd shut her out, his indifference eviscerating her heart.

But now she had to wonder… What if he hadn't been heartless? What if he really had cared? What if he'd believed that *just like his father,* she'd chosen her ambitions over him?

She inhaled sharply, her world upended at the thought. She might be jumping to conclusions. He'd never asked her to turn down that scholarship. He'd never asked her to stay. For all she knew, he might have been delighted to see her go. But if her father was right, and she'd hurt Cole…

Cole pocketed his cell phone. His gaze snagged hers from across the room, and the turmoil in her belly grew. He headed toward her, and she straightened, her emotions running amok.

Cole reached her side a second later. "I've called a meeting of the ranch hands," he told her father, his voice still raspy from inhaling smoke. "I told them to meet us in front of the house five minutes from now."

Her father nodded. "I'll wait outside." He balanced on his crutches and limped away.

Cole hesitated. His bloodshot eyes shifted to Bethany's, and she hugged her arms to quiet her nerves. "I need to talk to you after the meeting," he said.

"Sure." He turned to talk to the sheriff, and she studied his chiseled profile, wondering what he wanted to say. Still trying to corral her unruly emotions, she followed her father to the porch.

She spotted Ace curled up near the steps. The aging dog huddled against the railing, trembling from the commotion and noise. Knowing exactly how he felt, she knelt to give him a hug. She rubbed the top of his silky head, earning a grateful kiss in return, then buried her face in his fur. "It's okay," she whispered. "The fire's gone now."

And so were her illusions. Her sense of security had crumbled. Her certainty about the past had disappeared. She was even beginning to doubt her father's honesty—the man she'd always revered.

The cold wind gusted, bringing with it the stench of burnt wood. She gave Ace a final pat and rose, utterly drained. The ambulance pulled away from the house, carrying the mercenary's body to the county morgue—a grim reminder of the violence stalking the ranch.

Still feeling off balance, she joined her father in the yard. Several cowboys headed toward them—Earl Runningcrane, Bill, and Kenny Greene. Tony walked close behind them, and she struggled to hide her distaste.

A second later Cole tramped down the steps. He frowned as the remaining ranch hands roared past in their pickup trucks, heading toward the gate. "Where are they going?"

Earl shifted his weight and cleared his throat. "They quit. They've been complaining about the workload for a while now, and this murder was the final straw. They said they hadn't signed on for this."

Cole didn't answer. He just tipped back his head and closed his eyes.

Bethany's heart rolled. *Of all the times to lose his men.* She caught Kenny's eye, and he winced his sympathy. At least Cole still had a few good men.

"All right," Cole said. "I know you're all tired, but we need to get those calves loaded up. It will probably take us a couple of days now that we don't have as many men.

"I need to make some calls and get the insurance claims started, then I'll be out to help."

"What are we going to do for tack?" Tony asked.

"Good question." He rubbed his stubble-roughened jaw, then turned his gaze to Earl. "Check the old tack shed behind the bunkhouse. There might still be some gear in there. I'll see what I've got in the house. And make a list of what you've all lost so I can file a claim."

He paused, his voice turning to steel. "From now on, no one goes anywhere alone. You hear me? Do everything in pairs. And carry a weapon with you at all times. I'm making arrangements with the sheriff to increase their patrols, but in the meantime, watch your backs. Any questions?"

The men shook their heads. "Then let's get started. I'll be out as soon as I make those calls. Tony, you're in charge of loading the calves. Rusty, hold up a minute. I need to talk to you."

The men headed toward the bunkhouse, Domino and Mitzy at their heels. Bethany stood beside her father, surprised when Sheriff Colton joined their small group.

Cole glanced at the retreating cowboys, then turned to face them again. "I didn't want to say this in front of the men, but I'm beginning to think that someone on the inside could be involved in this."

Bethany's breath caught. She whipped her gaze to her father, but he stared back at Cole, his eyes shuttered, his craggy face like stone.

"That means we can't take any chances," Cole said. "At least until the sheriff has checked things out. Rusty, I want you to move into my house until you're off those crutches. Pack up some things, and I'll send someone over to get them."

His gaze honed in on Bethany's. "And I want *you* on the next flight back to Chicago."

"What? I can't leave." Not while her father was in danger. Not while a sinister society was threatening the ranch.

Sheriff Colton cleared his throat, drawing her gaze to him. "There was a note attached to the body."

Something in his tone evoked a shiver of dread. "What kind of note?"

He glanced at Cole, then swung his gaze back to her. "They've threatened to go after you next."

Dizziness barreled through her. She wobbled on her feet, and Cole lunged toward her and grabbed her arm. "Me?" She gaped from Cole to the sheriff in disbelief. "But…that's crazy. Why would they go after me? What do I have to do with this?"

The sheriff shook his head. "I don't know. It might be an idle threat. But we have to assume that it's real, given that they've already murdered a man."

"But—"

"We can't protect you here," Cole said. "We don't have the manpower or time. We don't even know who we're up against. You need to go back to Chicago where you'll be safe."

Suddenly chilled, she crossed her arms. She certainly didn't want to die. And Cole had enough on his mind without worrying about protecting her.

"There's no reason for you to risk your life," he added. "This isn't your fight. And Rusty will be fine in the house."

"Cole's right," her father said, his voice sober. "You need to go somewhere safe."

She struggled to absorb the revelation, to think through her burgeoning fear. They were probably right. She *should* go back to Chicago. Not only could she escape the danger, but she could investigate Mrs. Bolter's death and clear her name.

But no one was chasing her off this ranch. Not with so many unanswered questions. She owed it to Cole and her father to stay.

"You don't know that I'll be safer there," she argued. "A gunman can hide more easily in a crowd. At least here a stranger sticks out. And I don't mind carrying a gun."

"It might not be a stranger," Cole said, sounding grim.

She winced, knowing how much that had to hurt. "Even so, there's no guarantee Chicago will be any safer. They kidnapped Lana in Europe, right?"

Cole and the sheriff exchanged glances. Cole lowered his brows, obviously not thrilled to have her stay.

"I'll be careful," she added. "I won't take any risks."

Cole's steely eyes met hers. "All right, but only under one condition. You and your father are both moving into my house. You're going to stay in there with my father's bodyguards until this blows over. I mean it," he warned. "You're not leaving that house."

Her heart missed a beat. Protests crowded her throat. She'd be living in Cole's house, sharing his meals, aware of every movement he made. "But—"

"That's the rule. You either stay in the house with the bodyguards or return to Chicago tonight."

Their eyes held. Several tense seconds ticked past. Realizing he wouldn't budge, she lifted her hands. "Fine."

Cole's mouth tightened. "I'll tell Hannah to ready your rooms."

He turned and climbed up the porch steps. The sheriff took his leave, then headed to his patrol car across the yard.

Bethany trailed her father toward his cabin, her thoughts in disarray, her belly a jumble of dread. She had far more to worry about than resisting her attraction to Cole. Murderers threatened her life. Someone on Cole's ranch could be to blame.

And worse, if her father *did* know something about this, she couldn't conceal it from Cole, not with their lives at risk.

But how could she turn her father in?

Caught between opposing loyalties, she skirted a pile of ashes and choked back the acrid fumes. One thing was clear. If Cole believed she'd abandoned him once, she couldn't do it again.

No matter what the cost.

Chapter 8

Bethany gazed out the great-room window hours later, her thoughts still in turmoil, feeling as gutted as the demolished barn. Steel-bottomed clouds hung over the snow-capped mountains. A deep quiet gripped the ranch house, the methodical ticks of the clock on the fireplace mantel torturing her already pent-up nerves.

She still didn't want to believe she'd hurt Cole. All these years she'd been the injured one, self-righteous in her indignation over his rejection of her. But her insights into his father had shattered those beliefs. And for the first time, she had to consider the possibility that *she'd* acted badly—that she'd been so driven, so wrapped up in her goals and ambitions that she'd wounded the man she'd loved.

She shifted her weight, trying to steer her mind from that awful thought. Because an even more disturbing question lurked on the heels of that one: if Cole *had* asked her to stay in Montana, if he'd asked her to give up that scholarship and live in Maple Cove, what would she have done?

She pressed her hand to her belly, not anxious to answer that. Because if she did…she might not be as different from Cole's father as she'd thought.

Shying away from that unflattering possibility, she drew her sweater closer around her and searched for something to do. But Hannah had gone into town with Gage Prescott to pick up groceries. Both her father and the senator were taking naps. The house was already spotless, and Hannah would kill her if she interfered in her domain.

She could scrounge up some tack and help the men load up cattle—except she'd promised not to leave the house. But she couldn't stay cooped up inside with nothing to distract her; she would lose her mind.

She paced across the room to the stone fireplace, her restlessness increasing with every step. Hoping a friendly voice would help divert her, she pulled out her cell phone and speed-dialed Adam, but got his voice mail instead.

She tapped her fingers against the cell phone, his silence adding to her unease. It had been two days. He should have called with an update on Mrs. Bolter by now.

Unless he was trying to avoid her…

Rolling her eyes at that absurd thought, she dialed the nurses' desk at the Preston-Werner Clinic. The danger on the ranch was making her paranoid. She was inventing conspiracies where they didn't exist.

Besides, she didn't need to talk to Adam to learn the results of the investigation. The nurse on duty could put her uncertainties to rest.

"Hi, Janeen," she said when a nurse she worked with answered the phone. "It's Bethany."

"Oh. Hi, Bethany. What's up?" Janeen's overly chipper

voice—the one she used on patients when the news was bad—put Bethany on instant alert.

"I've been trying to find out about the investigation, what they've learned about Frances Bolter's death."

Janeen hesitated a beat, prompting another spurt of dread. "Didn't Adam phone you?"

"No. I just tried to call him but got his voice mail. So what did they find out?"

Janeen paused again, longer this time, and Bethany tightened her grip on the phone. "Hold on a minute," she said. "I…I've got another call."

She was lying. Bethany bit her lip, her nerves twisting higher as a pop song came over the line. But she drew in a steadying breath, determined not to overreact. Surely the clinic had cleared her of blame by now.

Janeen picked up the line a second later. "Sorry about that. Listen, Bethany. I can't…I'm not supposed to talk to you. Not while you're on administrative leave."

Her stomach swooped. "They put me on leave? No one told me that."

"Adam was supposed to notify you this morning."

Anxiety squeezed her throat and she struggled to breathe. "He might have tried. We just had a barn fire so there's been a lot of commotion here." Except her cell phone didn't show any missed calls. "But why would they put me on leave? I know I didn't—"

"I can't talk about it. I'm sorry."

"But they must have checked the reconciliation form by now and inventoried the drugs."

Janeen didn't answer, her silence damning. Bethany clutched the phone, panic mushrooming inside her, desperation threading her voice. "The inventory *must* have cleared me. I *know* I didn't give her the wrong dose. There has to be an ex—"

"I'm sorry. I can't say any thing more. I...I've got to go." Janeen disconnected the call.

Bethany didn't move, her mind reeling with disbelief. They'd suspended her from her job. They were investigating her. They thought she'd made a mistake that caused Frances Bolter's death.

She sank onto the sofa, her belly a tumult of dread. Could it be true? Might she have misjudged the dose? Horrified at the possibility, she pressed her hand to her lips. She'd been preoccupied about her father that night, in a hurry for her shift to end so she could pack for her trip.

But she was meticulous about dispensing drugs. She remembered entering the data on the reconciliation form and double-checking the dose. But then why didn't the form back her up? And why wasn't there enough of the study drug left to uphold her claim?

Then another terrible thought slammed into her, stealing her breath. *Maybe I need a lawyer.* Maybe they intended to charge her with negligence—or worse. But surely it wouldn't come to that. The autopsy *had* to support her claims. She hadn't done anything wrong.

But what if she had? What if she'd made a mistake that night...just as she'd misinterpreted the past with Cole?

Her stomach in total turmoil, she speared her hands through her hair. She couldn't sit here idly while everything she'd worked for collapsed. Nor could she leave; she'd vowed to stay in Montana until the threat to Cole and her father had passed.

Torn, she rose and stared out the window. The yard remained deserted; Cole would be busy loading cattle for hours. She could use his computer to access Frances Bolter's medical records and try to figure out what had gone wrong.

But as she headed down the hallway toward his office,

the irony of her situation struck her hard. She'd wanted to take her mind off Cole and put her conscience at ease.

Instead, her life had just gotten worse.

By nightfall Bethany had confirmed one thing. She was in one heck of a mess.

"Am I interrupting?"

Startled, she tore her gaze from the computer monitor and peered into the shadows dimming the room. Cole stood beyond the desk, the haze from the desk lamp accentuating the angles of his face. He'd showered recently, judging by his still-damp hair. A five o'clock shadow darkened his jaw.

Suddenly aware that she'd taken over his desk, she rose. "I'm sorry. I should have asked if I could use your computer. I wanted to look at my patient's medical records." She glanced at the now-black windows and winced. "Time obviously got away from me."

"I don't mind. You can use the computer whenever you want." His deep-toned voice sparked a surge of adrenaline, and her gaze swung back to him. She scanned his hard, masculine mouth, his broad shoulders encased in a white T-shirt, his flat abdomen and faded jeans. The intriguing stress spots in the denim made her face warm, and she jerked her eyes back up.

He held up a bottle of beer. "Join me in a beer? Or a glass of wine?"

She hesitated. She had no business spending time alone with Cole. He upset her equilibrium in too many ways.

He quirked a brow. "It's only a drink. And Hannah said dinner's not for half an hour."

Knowing that any excuse would look foolish, she released her breath. "Sure. Wine would be great."

"Wait here. I'll get it." He set his beer on the desk and

left. Struggling to gather her composure, she shut down the computer, picked up the pages she'd printed out, and tapped them into a pile. She could handle this. They'd have a drink. He'd tell her about the cattle; she would talk about her job. She didn't need to obsess about the past and analyze what she'd done wrong.

Cole returned a moment later with the wine and a glass. "You still drink chardonnay?"

"That's perfect."

He set down the wineglass and got to work on the cork. She stood beside him, eyeing the powerful curve of his biceps, the corded sinews in his tanned arms. His clean, soap scent invaded her senses, making her heart increase its beat.

He gave the corkscrew a final twist and tugged out the cork. "So what did you find out?"

Her thoughts swerved to her patient, and her anxiety came racing back. "I phoned the clinic. They've placed me on administrative leave. They still think I made a mistake."

He paused and caught her eye. "I thought they were going to check the drug log."

"They did." She rubbed her arms, suddenly chilled. "It shows that I administered the wrong dose. And the drug inventory backs that up."

His eyes stayed on hers. "But you don't believe it."

"No, I don't believe it." She couldn't have made such a horrific mistake.

"So the drug log is wrong." His expression thoughtful, he turned back to the desk and poured her a glass of wine. "How well do you know the people you work with?"

Her jaw slackened. "You think someone set me up?"

"Do you?"

"No, of course not. I can't even imagine that. They're my friends. We've worked together for years."

He raised a pointed brow—reminding her that someone on his ranch, someone he'd known and worked with for years, could be trying to destroy him, too. And suddenly, she understood how he felt, knowing that someone he considered a friend had abused his trust.

Did he think she'd betrayed him, too?

Unnerved by that terrible thought, she forced her mind back to her job. "Even if someone *did* want to set me up, I don't see how they could do it. We keep the drug log on a computer, and whenever we enter the data, it records the time and date."

"Someone who knows computers could get around that."

"But why would anyone bother? It doesn't make sense. Everyone loved Mrs. Bolter. No one wanted to see her dead." And Bethany didn't have any enemies that she knew.

His eyes still thoughtful, Cole handed her the wine. "They'll do an autopsy, right?"

"Yes, definitely. And it should clear me of any blame. But the results might not be available for a while, depending on the backload at the lab."

And in the meantime, her reputation would be ruined.

Lightheaded at the possibility, she sipped her wine. Then she trailed Cole to a small seating group by the windows, and sat across from him in a leather chair.

"What were you looking for online?" he asked.

Inhaling, she tried to regroup. "Mostly I looked at her records."

"Did you find anything?"

"Nothing obvious. But I went back as far as I could, and saw that she did a stint in rehab years ago. At least it seems that way. There was a reference in one of her charts… I'd have to do more digging to be sure. The oldest records are probably still on paper. But they would have been archived somewhere."

"Rehab for what?"

"Alcohol abuse. But Adam should have known about that. He gave everyone a physical before the trial began. He wouldn't have let her in if it wasn't safe."

Cole shifted his gaze to the window, as if turning that over in his mind. "Then what do you think caused her death? The drug?"

She shook her head. "They do all sorts of tests on the drugs before they go to human trials. They're usually pretty safe." She paused and frowned at her wine.

"Usually?" Cole prodded

Still hesitating, she met his eyes. "But you hear rumors sometimes, that pharmaceutical companies suppress things. There's big money involved, and a new drug for rheumatoid arthritis…" She inclined her head. "You can imagine how lucrative it would be.

"In any case, it's all conjecture. The drug, her former alcohol abuse—none of that might have mattered. They might not have had anything to do with her death."

"But they might."

"Maybe." She grimaced. "I'd need to do more research. What I really need is access to a database, the kind a university library would have."

His dark brows knitted. "Would Montana State have what you need?"

"Probably." And Bozeman was less than an hour away.

"If you need to talk to someone, I still know some professors there."

"You went to Montana State?"

"At night. It took me a while, but I got an agribusiness degree. I thought it might come in handy, particularly the accounting and finance parts. The fewer people I have to hire, the more money I can funnel back into the ranch."

She drained her glass, impressed. And suddenly, winning that full-ride scholarship didn't seem like such a great achievement. While she'd had the luxury of attending school full-time, Cole had earned his degree the hard way—after putting in long days at the ranch.

Cole took her empty glass and returned to the desk. Bethany studied his powerful back, the play and flex of his muscles under his shirt, and a heavy feeling unfurled in her chest. She'd always admired Cole's strength. He didn't shirk from a job, didn't lean on anyone else. The way he'd put himself through college epitomized that.

But maybe that self-reliance came from necessity. Maybe he'd learned that he *had* to go it alone.

And maybe she'd reinforced that belief when she left.

She dropped her gaze to her hands, a sudden thickness blocking her throat. She'd adored Cole. She couldn't stand the thought that she might have hurt him. Surely she hadn't been that self-involved.

"More wine?" he asked.

Thrown off-kilter, she met his gaze. She shouldn't linger. She should go back to her room and think this out, put some badly needed distance between them before she said something she would regret. But when had she ever done the logical thing around Cole?

"All right." She rose and joined him at the desk. While he poured her wine, she studied his rugged profile—his straight, masculine nose, the sexy downward slant of his cheekbones, the virile beard stubble shadowing his jaw. She'd been so crazy in love with this man, and she'd thought she'd known him so well. Could she really have misinterpreted what he'd felt?

His blue eyes skewered hers. Her pulse abruptly sped

up. She swallowed, suddenly far too aware of how close he stood. His warm, muscled arm brushed hers.

"How are the cattle?" she asked, her heart struggling to find a beat. "Did you get them all shipped off?"

"About half." He picked up his beer and leaned against the desk. "We'll finish the rest tomorrow morning and return the trucks to Butte. I'm heading up to the mountains after that."

"Do you know where the rest of the herd is?"

"Near the divide. Del took me up in his helicopter this afternoon to check. The good news is that the herd's intact." A crease formed between his brows. "I just hope the snow holds off. This first storm of the season is supposed to be a big one."

She nodded. A heavy snowfall could devastate the herd, cutting off their access to water and food. "Who are you taking with you?"

"Tony and Kenny Greene."

She wrinkled her nose. She didn't trust Tony; if anyone on this ranch was conspiring with killers, she'd put her money on him. But her predicament in Chicago had taught her one thing—it hurt to be accused of something you didn't do. And she couldn't inflict that same damage on anyone else—not her father, not even a despicable bully like Tony, not without concrete proof. She needed far more evidence than a forgotten scrap of leather or some thuds she'd heard in the barn.

"You'll need more than two people to help you if you've got a hundred head to bring in," she said. "Especially with that snow."

"I can't do anything about that. I need to leave Earl and Bill here to tend the rest of the herd."

"I'll go with you. I can go to Bozeman tomorrow morning

and do my research while you finish loading the cattle and return the trucks. I'll be back before you leave."

He shook his head. "Forget it. You agreed to stay in the house."

"I'll go crazy sitting around here."

"Better crazy than dead."

Her exasperation rose. "But I can't stay inside. I told you, I need to get to a university library."

"Why can't you look online?"

"It would take too long. I can't possibly search the online library of every university in the world. I need access to an index, a database like D.A.I.—Dissertations Abstract International. I can skim through that, and if a dissertation looks promising I can go from there. It's still a long shot, but at least it gives me a chance."

"Then wait until I get back. I'll only be gone a couple of days."

"I can't. My reputation will be ruined by then. I can't just sit here doing nothing while everything I've worked for falls apart."

Cole set down his empty bottle and sighed. "Bethany, be reasonable. You saw that note. They've threatened to go after you next."

Her breath hitched, apprehension clutching her chest. "I'll be careful. I promise. The library must have a metal detector. No one's going to barge in there with a gun."

"The hell they won't." He rose and turned to face her. "Don't you understand how dangerous this is? Those people just killed a mercenary."

"I know, but—"

"He was a *professional* and he died. You don't stand a chance."

"You're not sitting back while they attack your ranch."

His mouth hardened. "That's different."

"No, it's not."

"Of course it is. For God's sake, Bethany—"

"I'm going to do this. I have to, Cole." Her eyes pleaded with his. "If I hide in the house it means the bad guys win. And I've worked too hard for too many years to let this destroy me now."

He worked his jaw, as if striving for control, his eyes never wavering from hers. And a host of emotions paraded through his eyes—frustration, resignation, respect... And something deeper. Something that looked a lot like desire.

Her stomach swooped. She turned stock-still, unable to tear her gaze from his. And her traitorous mind bombarded her with sensual memories—the erotic rasp of his jaw, the hard feel of his muscled frame. That heady rush of delirium she'd felt when he'd moved his lips over hers.

Her mouth turned to dust. Cole's eyes darkened, igniting a blast of heat in her blood. She'd seen that hungry look too many times to mistake his intent.

She dropped her gaze to his mouth. She tried to swallow, but failed. He reached out and cupped her jaw, his warm, calloused hand sending thrills racing over her skin. She abruptly lost the capacity to think.

"Stay in the house," he said, his voice rusty. "It's a bad idea to go out."

So was this. But she couldn't move to save her life.

He stroked his thumb down her throat. She trembled, the soft touch making her quiver, desire skidding and streaming through her veins.

His Adam's apple dipped. He slid his hands to her shoulders and hauled her upright, pulling her body to his. She closed her eyes, the hard, hot feel of him sparking a torrent of need.

And then he lowered his head, fused his mouth to hers, and everything inside her went wild. Pleasure curled inside her. A craving throbbed deep in her womb. She ran her hands up his arms, glorying in the muscles bulging under her palms, shuddering at the splendor of his kiss.

He shifted and widened his stance, pulling her hips against his. His mouth ravaged hers, making her senses whirl, the thick, potent feel of him weakening her knees.

This was madness. Perfection. Bliss. She couldn't move, couldn't think, couldn't do more than yield to the staggering need. Urgency uncoiled inside her, the intense desire to strip off her clothes and feel the heaven of his hands making her moan.

"Cole, dinner's ready," Hannah called from the hallway.

He jerked up his head. His breath sawed in the air. His eyes burned into hers, almost angry in their intensity, and for one raw, unguarded moment, she saw the same naked yearning she knew he could see in hers.

But then a shield fell over his face. He dropped his hands and stepped back, his expression carefully blank. And she couldn't deny the truth. He was fighting this attraction. He didn't *want* to desire her. Whatever he'd once felt for her was gone.

Hurt twisted inside her, followed by regret. She'd caused that distrust. She'd ruined something special when she'd left. She'd caused pain to the man she'd loved. "Cole, I—"

"We'd better go. Hannah doesn't like dinner to get cold."

He was right. This wasn't the time to rehash the past. He started to stalk from the room.

"I really do need to go to Bozeman tomorrow," she said.

He stopped, stood with his back to her for several seconds, then swore and strode away.

She inched out a tremulous breath. Her hands trembling, she gathered the papers she'd printed out and clutched them to her chest.

She'd just confirmed one thing. Her father was right. She'd wounded Cole badly when she'd left.

But how she could repair it, she didn't know.

Chapter 9

He'd screwed up again, big-time.

Cole paced across his front porch in the darkness, battling to get his wired-up body under control. He never
should have touched her. He'd caved to a moment of in-
sanity and once again broken his vow. But the seductive
fragrance of her skin, the fire flashing in those temptress
eyes had been too much to resist.

Pulling away from her had been torture. Keeping his
eyes off her during dinner had tested the limits of his self-
control. The husky purr of her voice, the alluring sight of
her kiss-swollen lips had kept him painfully aroused. He'd
bolted down his meal, sure he'd offended her when he'd
rebuffed her attempts to talk. But he'd had no choice. He
either had to get out of the house or drag her back to his
bedroom and finish what they'd started with that kiss.

He reached the end of the porch, then started back
toward the door. He didn't need this distraction. Not now.

Not when killers had captured his sister. Not when they'd threatened Bethany's life.

So what if they had chemistry? So what if she fueled his erotic fantasies—and always had? He couldn't let down his guard, couldn't allow her to burrow beneath his defenses—a surefire path to pain.

The low rumble of an approaching vehicle caught his attention, and he stopped. He aimed his gaze at the gate, welcoming the distraction. Headlights swept the yard, illuminating the mounds of charred rubble that comprised his former barn, and then the sheriff's SUV came into view. It neared the house, its tires crunching on gravel. The sheriff cut the engine and climbed out.

"Evening, Cole." Wes Colton stomped up the porch steps, rubbing his hands. "Cold night to be standing outside."

He nodded. He'd needed a blast of frigid air to cool his blood. "Yeah, that front's moving in fast." He cocked his head toward the door. "Come on in."

"Thanks, but I can't stay. I just wanted to update you on what we've found out."

"Did you find any evidence? Any idea who killed Garrison?"

"No, it's still too soon for that. Those tests will take a couple of weeks. I ran the background check on your ranch hands, though."

Cole folded his arms and steeled himself for the news. "What did you find?"

"Not much, unfortunately. Tony Whittaker had a juvenile record, minor stuff—breaking and entering—but he's stayed out of trouble since then. Earl Runningcrane got into a bar fight a few years back and was arrested for disturbing the peace. He pleaded guilty and paid a fine. The rest are clean."

So they'd come up empty. "I guess it was worth a try."

"It doesn't mean they're not involved. I just don't have any evidence to indicate they are yet. I'll keep looking. I'm going to check their bank accounts, credit reports, see if any unusual activity pops up."

"I appreciate that." Cole paused. "Sure you don't want to grab a beer?"

"No, thanks. I'm going to do a loop around your ranch and head home. I'll let you know when I've got news, though."

"Thanks. By the way, I'll be gone for a couple of days. I still need to bring down some cattle from summer pasture. I'm leaving the day after tomorrow." Assuming nothing else went wrong.

The sheriff nodded. "I'll increase our patrols. Let me know when you get back." He tramped down the porch steps and got into his SUV.

His thoughts on his ranch hands, Cole stayed on the porch as the sheriff drove off, the low whine of his engine fading into the night. No matter how many ways he examined it, his conclusion was always the same. One of his hands had to be involved—someone who knew the ranch's daily routines. Someone who'd known when his men were gone. Someone who could move around freely—shutting down sprinklers, disabling the security system—without anyone catching on.

Someone who'd betrayed his hard-earned trust.

He crossed his arms, his mind veering back to Bethany—and the flickers of guilt he'd glimpsed in her eyes. But that was nuts. Bethany had nothing to do with the problems on his ranch. And he needed to keep it that way— which meant convincing her to forget the library. She needed to stay in the house where she'd be safe.

The cold wind gusted, hastening him into the house.

Unable to put off the confrontation with Bethany any longer, he headed down the carpeted hall of the guest wing, then rapped on her bedroom door.

She opened it a second later. Her cheeks were flushed. Damp tendrils of hair clung to her temples and neck. His gaze dropped from her full, sensual mouth to the loose T-shirt that stopped halfway down her thighs. She clutched a towel to her chest.

His breathing suddenly uneven, he forced his gaze back up. But her sweet, feminine scent curled around him. Her straight black hair gleamed like silk in the hazy light. He couldn't move, paralyzed by the memory of her soft, supple body, the delirium of her mouth.

Did she have anything on underneath that shirt?

He cleared his throat. "We need to talk about tomorrow."

Her eyes turned wary. "What about it?"

Still trying not to imagine her naked, he kept his gaze on her face. "I know you want to go to the library in Bozeman, but—"

"I don't *want* to go there, I *have* to. I can't sit around here doing nothing while my career gets destroyed. I have to fight back, Cole. I can't take this lying down."

She raised her chin—a gesture he knew well. And a sinking feeling took hold inside. He'd never make her stay in the house. The minute he left to load up his cattle, she'd hop in a car and go. And he couldn't blame her. In her place, he would do the same.

"Then how about if we compromise?"

"Compromise how?"

"You're probably right about the library," he conceded, although the idea still filled him with misgivings. "You'll be safe with people around. We just need to get you there and back."

Her forehead crinkled. She chewed her bottom lip, the move drawing his gaze to her lush mouth, bringing a jolt of heat to his loins. "What do you suggest?"

That you strip off that shirt right now.

He squeezed the bridge of his nose, trying to banish the thought. "We should finish loading the cattle by noon. I can go with you to Bozeman while my men return the trucks."

She shook her head, and her long, silky hair slithered over her slender arms. "I can't wait that long. The research could take all day. And it's a terrible waste of time for you."

That was true. He already had enough to do to get ready for the trip. "So I'll help you do your research."

"You can't. I don't even know what I'm looking for exactly. And there's really no need. I can drive myself."

"It's too risky. What if someone follows you there?"

She tapped her bare foot. Frustration brewed in her eyes. "Then how about this? I heard Gage say he was going into Maple Cove for breakfast. How about if he follows me to the highway and makes sure there isn't a problem? Once I'm out of town, no one will know where I've gone."

Cole turned that over in his mind. It still made him nervous, but it was better than letting her head off alone. "All right, providing Gage approves the plan. And call me when you're ready to come back. I'll meet you at the highway and escort you back to the ranch."

"Fine, but I have a condition of my own." She paused. "I'm going to the mountains with you."

"Forget it."

She huffed out her breath. "Cole, come on. That front's moving in. You've seen the reports. You're going to need help up there when it starts to snow."

She was right. Driving a hundred head of cattle down the mountain during a snow storm was no mean feat.

Horses and cattle could slip. Conditions could turn deadly fast. And even if they managed to get the cattle loaded without a mishap, the trucks could roll on the icy roads.

But he had no business involving her in his problems. Bad enough that his sister was in danger. He couldn't risk Bethany's life, too. And if one of his men really was involved and followed them into the hills...

"I'll handle it," he said.

"You'll handle it better if I'm there to help. Besides, you said you don't want me going anywhere alone, so I'll go with you. Then you can keep me safe."

Safe? He snorted. She had no idea the effort it was costing him to keep his hands off her. And working—sleeping—in close quarters for days on end would strain his self-control.

But the bodyguards had their hands full trying to keep his father in line. He couldn't ask them to ride herd over Bethany, too.

"I'll be careful," she said. "I'll carry a gun. And you need the extra hand."

A feeling of defeat seeped through him. "It's not going to be a pleasant trip."

"It won't be the first time I've camped out."

Their eyes met. Awareness coursed between them. And he knew she was remembering the same thing he was— the cattle drive they'd made with his uncle Don.

Only they'd done things far more interesting than rounding up cows.

Heat bolted straight to his groin. His breath turned shallow and fast. He devoured the feminine swell of her lips, the pulse point at the hollow of her throat, her nipples pebbling under her shirt.

She moistened her lips. Her erotic scent twined around him, reeling him in like a siren's song. And it took all his strength to keep from ripping off that shirt, hauling her naked body into his arms, and sating the heavy urges laying waste to his self-control.

"Cole," she whispered, and the soft sound flayed him like a whip.

"Close the door," he ground out. His voice sounded dragged from a cave.

Her hot gaze stayed on his. For an eternity she didn't move.

"Bethany, close the damned door *now*."

"Right." A dull stain flushed her cheeks, and she stepped back. "I-I'll see you tomorrow." She shut the door in his face.

He stayed rooted in place, his blood bludgeoning his skull, so aroused he couldn't move. He braced his hands on the doorjamb, wrestling with the need to shoulder open that door and finish what they'd started with that kiss.

But he couldn't touch her. He couldn't surrender to this primitive hunger, no matter how hot she made him burn. He'd already learned the hard way that she would cause him nothing but pain.

But as he stalked slowly back to his bedroom, he knew one thing. That trek with her into the mountains would be the longest ordeal of his life.

She'd seriously lost her mind.

Bethany hunched at a computer terminal at the Montana State University library the following afternoon, so wound up she wanted to scream. Instead of concentrating on her research, her mind kept gravitating to Cole—his rumbling voice, his hungry eyes, the incredible ecstasy of his kiss. She'd spent the entire night reliving every sound, gesture and move he'd made, so on fire she couldn't sleep.

And it had to stop. She had too much work to do to be

acting like a lovesick fool. So Cole was hot. So the man could incinerate steel with a kiss. There were plenty of attractive men in Chicago willing to take her out, and she wasn't obsessing about them.

But pitting those men against Cole was like comparing a vintage black-and-white movie to high-definition TV. They weren't even in a similar league.

But no matter how masterfully Cole kissed—even if one carnal look from those dazzling blue eyes sent her into a torrent of need—she couldn't blind herself to the facts. They hadn't resolved the past. They had vastly different goals in life. And Cole didn't want her. He'd closed right down after that torrid kiss, firmly shutting her out.

She sighed and massaged her eyes, gritty from staring at the computer all day, and tried to subdue her traitorous mind. She had to think about Cole later. She had to focus on her research and figure out why Frances Bolter had died. This could be her only chance.

Forcing her attention back to the computer, she scrolled through another dissertation on an experimental drug. She skimmed through the technical jargon, decided it wasn't what she needed, then skipped to the next one on her list.

Still struggling to focus, she glanced at the abstract, which looked promising, then paged down to the summary at the end. The drug was similar to Rheumectatan, the one they were testing. But it had been linked to renal failure, causing the researchers to abandon the trials. That side effect had been even more pronounced when the patient had a history of alcohol abuse.

She straightened, her interest suddenly caught. Returning to the start, she read the article slowly, her excitement mounting with every word. She minimized the screen, skimmed through reports on the effects of renal failure, convinced she was on the right track. Several articles later, she came across a study linking kidney dysfunction in post-menopausal women to sudden cardiac death.

Her heart racing, she sat back. Frances Bolter was the right age. And if she'd been an alcoholic, the drug could have damaged her kidneys, leading to her sudden death. But then why had Adam approved her for the trial? Unless he hadn't known...

Bethany tugged on her lip, trying not to jump to conclusions or overreact. It was just one study. The drugs involved might not be as similar as she thought. Or outside factors might have influenced the results, voiding the conclusion she'd reached. But if she *was* right...just *maybe* she could clear her name.

She closed her eyes, dizzy with relief. But then another thought occurred to her, and she sat bolt upright again. If this study applied to Rheumectatan, other conditions besides alcoholism could trigger the same results. They needed to halt their trial before another patient died.

She paged through the article, checked the copyright disclaimer, making sure it was legal to copy for educational use. Then she emailed a copy to Adam at his private address. That done, she tossed on her jacket, gathered her papers and purse and hurried to the exit, feeling as if a boulder had been lifted from her back. She couldn't get too excited—the research might not pan out—but for the first time in a week she had hope.

She pushed through the library doors, then paused, surprised that it had turned dark. She glanced at her watch. *Nearly seven.* She had to hurry. She'd spent more time in the library than she'd thought.

A cold gust of wind blasted past. Shivering, she zipped up her jacket and raised the collar, then started toward the visitors' parking lot where she'd left her dad's truck. A group of students scurried by, squealing when the brisk wind hit their backs.

Anxious to tell Adam about her discovery, she dialed him on her cell phone, hoping that he'd pick up.

He did. "Hey, Bethany," he said. "I'm on another line. Can I call you right back?"

"Sure, but make it quick. I just discovered something you need to hear."

"Give me ten minutes."

"I'll talk to you then." She disconnected the call, shuddering when a spattering of icy raindrops hit her face. She jogged across Grant Street to the parking lot. Halogen light gleamed off the vehicles, the silver sheen a reminder of the coming snow.

Hurrying even more now, she closed the distance to the truck. Once inside, she cranked up the heater, blowing on her hands while she waited for the engine to warm.

She'd just backed out of her parking space when her cell phone rang. "Sorry about that," Adam said.

"That's okay." She shifted into gear and left the lot. "Listen. I've got great news. I did some research today at Montana State University and found a dissertation that might explain Mrs. Bolter's death."

"How so?"

Maneuvering through campus and back toward the highway, she summarized what she'd found, including Mrs. Bolter's possible alcohol abuse. "I just emailed you a copy of the dissertation," she added. "I need you to look it over and see what you think. They did the study here at Montana State, so I can contact the advisor if you've got questions. I can't do it for a couple of days, though. I'm heading to the mountains tomorrow to help round up some stranded cows."

"You're becoming quite the cowgirl."

The sarcasm in his voice brought her up short. "This *is* how I grew up."

"Hey, I was joking. I didn't mean it as an insult."

Suspecting she'd overreacted, she sighed. "I know. I'm sorry. I'm just tired." She'd spent too many sleepless hours anguishing over Cole. "Listen, if I'm right about this, you have to tell the study director. They need to halt the study before anyone else gets hurt."

"That's a bit extreme, don't you think?"

"Not if it saves someone's life. My God, Adam. Any number of patients could have problems we didn't screen for. What if—"

"All right. All right! I believe you. Don't have a coronary. I'll give the report to Marge and suggest we stop the trial."

"Fine." Mollified, she pulled in a breath. But it still rankled that he hadn't instantly understood the danger. How could he be willing to take a risk? Unless he was more involved in this than she knew...

Okay. Now she was *really* losing it. Adam had no reason to sink her career. His recommendation had helped her get the job.

She stopped at a traffic light and sighed. "Thanks, Adam. I might be wrong, but I don't think so. I have a feeling about this."

"We can't take the chance regardless. Patient safety has to come first."

"I knew you'd see it that way. I wish everyone did. If the administration hadn't cut our funding we could have rolled out that new bedside medication system by now, and I wouldn't be in this mess."

"Maybe this case will spur them to fund it."

"That would be great." Then maybe some good would

come of Mrs. Bolter's death. "I just wish they weren't blaming me for this."

"Don't worry. We'll get it straightened out."

"I hope so." The light changed, and she took the turn for the highway. "I've got to go. I'm nearly on the highway. But be sure to watch for that email."

"I'll take care of it as soon as I get home," he promised.

Bethany ended the call, then merged onto the highway, her hopes cautiously buoyed. This study didn't vindicate her completely. She still had to figure out why the drug reconciliation form and inventory were wrong. But it was a major start.

More sleet gathered on the windshield, and she turned her intermittent wipers on. Then a cattle truck roared past, reminding her of the upcoming trip to the mountains—and that she'd promised to telephone Cole.

Her heart beating fast, she dialed the ranch, then grimaced in disgust. She was definitely acting like a giddy schoolgirl, falling apart at the thought of Cole.

"Bar Lazy K," he said. She shivered, his deep, gravelly voice sounding far too intimate in the dark.

"It's me, Bethany. I just got on the highway. I should reach Maple Cove in about twenty-five minutes or so."

"I'll head to the highway now."

"You'd better wait. The roads are slick so I'm driving pretty slow. I'll phone again when I get to the pass."

"All right. Be careful."

"I will." Her voice came out breathless, and she stifled a sigh. This was beyond ridiculous. She had to get a grip before she made a total fool of herself.

Cole might still physically desire her, but he'd made it clear he didn't want an affair—which was good. Between their past and the current danger, they didn't need the complication of sex.

Especially if her father was involved with the sabotage at the ranch.

Dread pooled inside her. She'd been skirting that possibility for days, but it was time she faced it head-on. And the bottom line was…she still refused to believe that her father would ever harm Cole. He just didn't have it in him. And what motive could he possibly have?

Still, she knew he was hiding something. But what? Her father got along with everyone. He was the most accommodating person she knew. He never antagonized anyone, never lost his temper, even when provoked. He'd even endured years of racial prejudice so her mother could live in Maple Cove.

Turning that over in her mind, she passed a slow-moving truck, still unable to connect the dots. Then out of nowhere came a sudden thought. What if her father really hadn't done anything bad—but he'd seen someone else harming the ranch? And what if that someone—such as Tony—had threatened him to make sure he didn't talk?

Electrified, she tightened her grip on the wheel. That made far more sense. Her father might not confront a bully. And she could certainly envision Tony intimidating an elderly man.

But if it was true, it made her dilemma worse. She couldn't hide her suspicions from Cole. He had a right to know what was happening on his ranch. If she didn't speak up, and he found out later, he'd see her silence as a betrayal, an unforgivable breach of trust.

But neither could she implicate anyone—even Tony—without proof.

She turned up the speed on her wipers, her mind whirling through options, but she could only see one way out. If her father refused to talk, then it was up to her to find some proof. She would corner Tony in the mountains, show him that bridle browband, and force him to confess his part—before anyone else got killed.

Certain she was on the right track now, she flicked on the radio, picking up a station out of Bozeman, then hummed along to a country song. She kept an eye on the edge of the highway in case a deer or elk decided to cross the road.

The traffic slowed as she neared the pass. She tapped on the brakes, hoping no one had suffered an accident on the icy roads, then exhaled as they came to a stop. Suddenly feeling the lack the sleep, she yawned and rubbed her eyes.

Then a car zipped past on the shoulder and exited to the country road just ahead. She frowned, thinking fast. If she left the highway, she could pick up the old gravel road that angled south toward the ranch. It took longer to drive than the highway, but if this traffic stayed stopped for long…

Making a quick decision, she pulled onto the shoulder and followed the other car. A pickup swung in behind her as she drove down the exit ramp. It stayed on her bumper as she turned onto the country road.

She lowered the volume on the radio and reached for her cell phone, figuring she'd better let Cole know that she'd changed her route—but the glare in her rearview mirror made it hard to see. She squinted at the side mirror. The idiot behind her had his high beams on—and he was tailgating her like mad.

The road narrowed, and began to curve. She eased off on the pedal and hugged the shoulder, trying to give him room to pass. She didn't need some yahoo riding her bumper all the way to the ranch.

But he slowed and stayed behind her. Alarm prickling through her, she swung back out and sped up—and he kept pace. Sweat moistened her upper lip. Foreboding breathed down her spine. What was his problem? Was he drunk? Trying to be obnoxious? Or something worse?

She slowed again, and so did he. She punched down hard on the accelerator, and he did the same.

Her heart began to thud. Trying to see him better, she flicked a gaze at the side view mirror, but the bright lights obliterated her view.

Her tires drummed in time to her heartbeat. Her palms grew slick on the wheel. The memory of the dead mercenary slashed through her mind, and she fought back an onrush of dread. Her cell phone rang, but she didn't dare try to answer. A second of inattention could send her careening off the mountain road.

The truck roared up behind her. She bit back a scream as he rammed her bumper hard. She swerved, then fishtailed wildly. Her heart thundering, she grabbed the gyrating wheel and managed to straighten the truck.

Panting, sweat stinging her eyes, she glanced in the rearview mirror. But he zoomed up behind her again. Desperate to outrun him, she flattened the accelerator to the floorboard, and sped toward the upcoming curve.

But the truck pulled even beside her. She shot a glance at the guardrail, stark fear making her numb. He was going to force her off the road.

They neared the curve. She stomped on the brakes, praying she didn't go into a skid. He shot ahead, just as another car approached head-on and blared its horn.

A wild sound formed in her throat. Her pursuer swerved back to the right, and the other car flew safely past. But her pursuer overcorrected and hit the guardrail. A terrible screech rent the air. She watched, horrified, as he veered all over the road, then somehow regained control. He disappeared around the bend.

She jerked to a halt, slamming her head back against the headrest. Wheezing, so panicked she could barely function, she executed a three-point turn. Then she pushed down hard on the pedal and raced back the way she'd come.

Within seconds, she zoomed up behind the car her attacker had nearly hit head-on. She swung out and passed him, and the driver lay on his horn.

"Sorry. Sorry." She knew she was driving like a maniac, but she had no choice. She raced toward the highway, struggling to stay on the winding road.

And hoped that she'd survive.

Chapter 10

Bethany drove through the gates of the Bar Lazy K a short time later, her heart banging against her rib cage, still struggling to catch her breath. She pulled up to the ranch house and braked, then pried her fingers from the steering wheel, so relieved she wanted to weep.

She'd done it. She'd outrun her would-be killer and made it safely back to the ranch. But now came the hardest part—hiding the attack from Cole.

Her hands trembling, she scooped up the articles she'd printed in the library. Then she climbed from the truck and waited for him to park beside her, her wobbly legs threatening to collapse. She gulped in the freezing air, determined to get her shattered nerves under control.

Because she'd realized something during that terrifying drive back to Maple Cove. She despised being a victim. She hated experiencing this horrific fear. And no way was she going to let some thug intimidate her into cowering inside the house.

Especially if the culprit was Tony. Bad enough that he'd bullied her during grade school. Bad enough that he'd threatened her in that note. But she refused to let him scare her. She would *not* show any fear.

Of course, she couldn't prove that he'd tried to attack her. *Yet.* But she'd get that proof in the mountains.

Assuming she could conceal the attack from Cole.

Cole climbed from his truck and headed toward her. She preceded him up the porch steps, the steady thuds of his footfalls a contrast to the frenzied beats of her heart. She scooted inside the house, the warmth wrapping around her like an embrace.

She closed her eyes and swayed, the horror of the attack threatening to demolish her hard-won control. But she couldn't let her mind wander back there. Not yet. Not until she'd made it to the privacy of her bedroom—and convinced Cole that nothing was wrong.

"How did it go?" he asked from behind her.

Fine, until someone tried to kill her.

She inhaled deeply and turned to face him. His blue eyes locked on hers—and she had the strongest urge to blurt out the truth.

Instead, she hugged her papers to her chest. "Good, actually. I found an unpublished dissertation that might explain Mrs. Bolter's death. I-I'll tell you about it tomorrow when we've got more time."

His shrewd eyes narrowed on hers. He cocked his head, like a hunting dog scenting the wind.

"I sent it to Adam," she continued. "The dissertation, I mean. I just called him, too… It's complicated, but—"

"Bethany."

"What?"

"What happened?"

Her chest squeezed. "What do you mean?"

His eyes holding hers, he stepped closer. He reached out and lifted her chin.

"You're rambling. You're shaking. And you're pale enough to collapse."

"I'm fine."

"Baloney." His voice held a hint of steel.

She steadied her gaze, trying furiously to project an aura of innocence—because no way could she tell him the truth.

Cole let out a hiss and dropped his hand. "For God's sake, Bethany, there's a killer on the loose. If something happened, I need to know."

Desperation surged inside her. She didn't want to lie—but he wasn't giving her much choice. "Nothing happened. I told you, I'm fine. Now can we please drop this? I'm tired. I'm hungry, and I need to pack for our trip. I assume we're getting an early start."

For an eternity, he didn't move. Frustration blazed in his eyes. She struggled to keep her composure, feeling sick about her deception, hoping she could beg his forgiveness later for having lied.

"We leave at six." Anger laced his voice. He turned on his heel and crossed the room.

Her throat closed up. She clutched her papers closer, appalled that she'd hurt him more.

"Cole." He paused, and his furious eyes cut to hers. "I—thanks for coming to get me. I appreciate it. And I-I'll tell you what I found out tomorrow."

His mouth flattened. Hostility rolled off him in waves. "Forget it. It's none of my business what you do." He pivoted on his heel and stalked away.

She closed her eyes, her stomach a jumble of guilt.

She hadn't meant to hurt him. But she couldn't tell him the truth. Not yet. Not until she'd found proof of Tony's involvement and could clear her father of guilt. And she could only do that if she accompanied them into the mountains to get those cows.

But as his angry strides receded, the pit in her belly grew. Instead of convincing Cole to forgive her for the past, she'd just made everything worse.

The morning dawned dull and gray, the leaden clouds hanging low over the mountains, sudden bursts of flurries presaging the heavier snow to come. Bethany slumped in the passenger seat of Kenny's truck, the dismal skies reflecting her mood.

She'd angered Cole. He'd barely looked at her while they'd loaded the horses. And when he did glance her way, the distance in his eyes made her heart freeze, proving she'd erased any progress she'd made.

The mountain road curved ahead. She caught a glimpse of Cole's pickup, his horse trailer hitched to the back, and couldn't quite stifle her sigh. She was beginning to think she couldn't do anything right around that man.

"You all right?" Kenny asked.

"Sure." The switch-backing road turned steeper. Kenny downshifted, his powerful truck handling the curves with ease, even with the gooseneck trailer in tow. She glanced his way, realizing she'd been so wrapped up in her thoughts of Cole that she'd hardly spoken on the two-hour drive.

"Sorry I'm not good company. I guess I'm a little preoccupied these days."

Kenny slid her a glance. "Is Tony still bothering you?"

"You noticed?"

He shrugged. "He's always been a jerk. He used to get

in my face, too. He doesn't bother me much anymore, though."

Bethany's mouth edged up. "Not since you've grown, huh?"

He smiled back. "Yeah." Kenny had been a thin, puny kid during grade school—a bully's easy prey. "I took boxing lessons, too. That helped. I landed a right hook to his nose once, and after that he left me alone. Ever notice that crook in his nose?"

She laughed. "Good work."

Still grinning, Kenny turned his eyes back to the road. But his words lingered, making her think. She hadn't been Tony's only victim. He'd pushed his weight around since childhood, tormenting vulnerable kids. Had he moved on to more sinister acts as an adult? It certainly appeared that way.

But she still needed proof.

Seconds later, Kenny turned off the road at Cole's corrals. Bethany shrugged on her sheepskin vest and grabbed her gloves. From here on out, they'd ride on horseback. Once they found the missing cattle they'd drive them back here and ship them out.

Kenny came to a stop. "You might as well get out here," he said. "I'm going to back the trailer in."

"All right." She hopped out and pulled on her gloves, her breath turning to frost in the air. Cole turned away as she headed toward him, and her stomach fell. So his temper still hadn't cooled.

She waited beside him and Tony, rubbing her arms to stay warm. They'd hauled their tack and three of their horses in Kenny's spacious, slant-load trailer. But Tony's roan gelding had proven so difficult to load—even trying to bite them—that they'd finally stuck him in a smaller trailer alone.

"All right," Cole said when Kenny joined them. "Let's get to work. Bethany, you help Tony unload his gelding. Kenny and I'll take care of the rest."

She nodded, her stomach balling at his clipped tone. How much angrier would he become when he found out about her dad?

Deciding not to borrow trouble, she turned her attention to the job at hand. Tony swaggered toward her, his pale eyes glinting with malice. A mottled bruise discolored his jaw.

Her pulse hitched. She turned toward the trailer, but gave him a sideways look. If he'd tried to run her off the road last night, he might have a bruise like that. When his truck had slammed against the guardrail, he could have banged his jaw.

She opened the trailer's back doors, trying to sound off-hand. "Interesting bruise you've got. What happened?"

He grunted. "I was in a fight."

"Really? Who with?"

His eyes narrowed. "Why do you care?"

"I don't. I was just curious." She pulled down the ramp, then aimed her gaze at him. "Someone tried to run me off the road last night."

He planted his hands on his hips. His mean eyes focused on hers. "Are you accusing me of something?"

"Not at all." This wasn't the time to press for answers, not when they had to unload his horse. But sometime during this trek through the mountains she intended to get the truth.

A thud in the trailer made her frown. His gelding was already raising a ruckus, stomping and trying to get out.

"You know," she said. "If you took the time to get your horse used to the trailer, he wouldn't be such a problem to load."

"He isn't a problem. You just need to know how to control him."

Her mouth flattened. Bullying didn't work with horses any more than it did with people. "You wouldn't have to use force if you'd just work with him a bit."

"He's my horse. I can treat him however I want."

Her temper rising, she bit back a reply. She couldn't stand men like Tony, who masked their inadequacies with force. She'd learned from her father—a true horseman—that consistency and patience gentled even the most skittish horse.

"I'll get the lead on him," she said. "Hold on."

Still seething, she stalked to Cole's truck and took out the lead rope, then headed to the trailer's escape door along the side. Tony's gelding continued to butt the partition and stomp his hooves.

She climbed up on the stoop and opened the window. Then she reached for the gelding's halter, needing to attach the lead rope before she unclipped the trailer tie. But before she could grab it, Tony leaped onto the loading ramp and unhooked the restraining strap from behind the horse.

"Wait a minute," she called. "I'm not ready. I don't have the lead rope on."

But with the strap suddenly gone, the horse sensed freedom. He instantly surged backward and thrashed his head. Bethany lunged for his halter again, but missed.

"Whoa, boy," she said, trying to calm him. But the gelding pinned back his ears and pulled again.

"Settle down. Settle down." Moving slowly so she wouldn't spook him, she inched her hand toward the anxious horse. But he whipped his head and jerked back. Without warning, the quick release on the halter snapped.

Her heart stopped. The horse began to rush back.

"Watch out!" she shouted to Tony. "He doesn't have the lead rope on."

But Tony ignored her warning. He climbed inside the trailer, and everything inside her froze. "What are you doing?" Didn't he know how dangerous that was? "Get out of there!"

"Shut up. I know how to manage my horse." Tony squeezed along the partition, muscling his way toward the front. The panicked gelding continued backward. His hind legs reached the ramp, and he started to swing around. Tony made a grab for the halter, but the horse's momentum bumped him back.

The impact knocked him off balance. He slipped and fell beneath the horse. Horror fisted inside her. *Oh, God. He was going to get crushed.*

Freaked by the sudden commotion, the horse sprang back—but Tony was in his way. His hoof landed on Tony's foot.

A sickening crack rent the air, and Tony screamed.

Swearing, Bethany jumped off the stoop and raced around the trailer. Cole sprinted over to help. "What happened?"

"Tony."

The horse leaped sideways off the ramp. Bethany dove for his halter, but he escaped her, then cantered toward the trees. She let him go, knowing they could catch him later on. Tony's injuries might not wait.

She hopped onto the ramp ahead of Cole and rushed to Tony's side. He lay sprawled on the floor, half crumpled against the partition, moaning and clutching his leg.

Her stomach fell away. Even from a distance, she could see the unnatural angle of his foot.

She knelt beside him, keeping her voice calm. "Lie back and stay still. Let me see what we've got."

"Leave me alone."

"I'm a nurse. Let me see."

His mouth thinned. "I don't need your help. Get your filthy hands off me."

Her face heating, she checked the size of his pupils, then scanned his scalp for bumps. She had a professional duty to help him, no matter how despicable he was. "Did he kick your head?"

"No."

"Too bad," she muttered. Anyone dumb enough to get into the trailer with an unrestrained horse…

He groaned and rolled to his side. "Stay still," she said again, her voice sharper. "Moving around is going to make it worse."

"I don't need some damned Indian ordering me around."

"You'll listen to this one," Cole said, the threat of violence in his voice. "And you'll watch your mouth—or I'll break a hell of a lot more than your foot."

Tony shut his mouth, but his eyes turned sulky. Bethany spared Cole a grateful glance. "We need the first aid kit."

"I'll get it." His jaw rigid, Cole shot Tony a warning look, then hurried off. Bethany picked up Tony's wrist and checked his pulse.

Cole reappeared a second later with Kenny in tow. "We need to cut his boot off before his foot starts to swell," she told them. "His pant leg, too, up to his knee so we can expose the wound."

Cole pulled out his pocketknife. While he and Kenny got to work, she rummaged through the first aid kit. Cole peeled away Tony's boot, then made short work of the sock. When they finished, Kenny scooted aside, and she took his place.

She swallowed hard. Tony definitely had a compound fracture. His foot dangled at a ghastly angle, and was already beginning to swell. "Can you wriggle your toes?" she asked him.

Grunting, a sheen of sweat breaking out on his forehead, he complied.

"Good. Now don't look at me." She waited until he averted his gaze, then squeezed his toe. "Which toe am I touching?"

"The little one," he gritted out.

She met Cole's eyes, relieved. "That's good. No obvious nerve damage. We need to immobilize the leg. Do you have something we can use as a splint?"

"I've got a board in the trailer," Kenny said.

"Good. Grab a saddle blanket for padding. And bring some wrapping tape to tie it down." While he darted away to get it, Bethany grabbed the scissors from the first aid kit.

Kenny returned a second later. "This is the tricky part," she told Cole. "I need you to help me lift his leg. Kenny, fold the blanket on the board, then slide it under his leg when we lift it up."

She aimed her gaze at Tony. "It's going to hurt, but you'll feel better when we're done."

She and Cole knelt across from each other. Kenny readied the board. She nodded to Cole. "Now." They raised his leg, and Tony cried out. Kenny slid the board in place. "Okay, lower it slowly," she said.

That done, she grabbed the tape and scissors. "We need to tie it in place. As soon as I cut some strips off, I'll need you two to lift the board."

She worked quickly to secure the board, then tied off the final knot. "Let me check for sensation again." She got Tony to wriggle his toes, made sure he could feel her touch.

Relieved, she sat back on her heels and released her breath. "That's all I can do. He needs a doctor now."

"We'll lie him in the backseat of your truck," Cole said to Kenny. "You've got more room than I do. You'll have to drive him to the hospital in Honey Creek."

The men hoisted Tony from the trailer, his moans filling the air. Bethany scrambled out behind them, then raced to Kenny's truck and opened the doors. She entered from the other side, cleared her gear from the backseat, then tugged her pillow from her sleeping roll.

The men laid him across the seat. She handed the pillow to Cole. "Put this under his leg to elevate it. And here's the cold pack."

Cole turned to Kenny. "We need to catch Tony's horse and put him in the trailer with yours. Let's just hope that damned gelding cooperates this time."

Kenny scowled, obviously not thrilled with the change of plans, but didn't argue. While the men left to catch the horse, Bethany stayed at Tony's side. "You all right?" she asked, checking his pulse again.

"Yeah." He paused. His eyes flicked to hers, then veered away. "Thanks."

She nodded, knowing it cost him to be polite. She skimmed her gaze over him again to make sure she hadn't overlooked any injuries, lingering on his bruised jaw. "Tell me about that bruise."

"Why?"

"I told you. Someone followed me last night and tried to run me off the road. His truck hit the guardrail, and the impact probably gave him a bruise like that."

"It wasn't me."

"Can you prove that?"

His eyes flashed. "Yeah, I can prove it. I was at the Wagon Wheel Saloon until midnight. Everyone saw me there. If someone tried to run you off the road, it wasn't me."

She frowned at that. His story would be easy to check. "Then what about this?" She pulled the browband from her pocket and held it out. "Care to explain how it got in the field by the dead cows?"

"How should I know?"

"Because it's yours."

"It is not. I've never seen it before."

"I don't believe you."

"You're nuts. What…?" Understanding dawned in his eyes. "You think I killed those cows."

"You bet I do."

"I had nothing to do with that."

She leaned closer. "Then who did?"

"How should I know?"

"Because you're the one causing the problems. And you threatened my father to stop him from turning you in."

"The hell I did. You're out of your mind."

She held his gaze. He glared back, denial hot in his eyes. And sudden doubts crawled through her mind. Even though she despised him, he seemed to be telling the truth.

But if he hadn't caused the problems…

The tailgate on the trailer slammed. Cole returned to the truck, and she stepped back, confusion muddling her mind. Kenny leaped into the driver's seat and started the engine while Cole closed Tony's door. They slowly drove away.

Bethany stared at the empty road, her world suddenly tossed on its head. If Tony had told her the truth, then she'd misjudged him. She'd let her childhood memories blind her to the facts.

Her stomach dipped. Her sense of superiority disappeared. She'd always considered herself fair-minded. She'd prided herself on her unbiased judgment, railing against bigotry in any form. But she'd been just as prejudiced against Tony, allowing her resentment to cloud her thinking, even creating a vendetta against him.

Which didn't make her any better than him.

The cold wind gusted. Chilled now, she met Cole's gaze, and another realization hit her hard. She never should have lied to Cole. If she'd told him about the attack, he could have taken precautions to keep them safe.

Because if Tony wasn't to blame, someone else was—and they'd just lost the only backup they had. They were now open targets, heading into the wilderness alone, a killer hard on their heels.

"Let's go," Cole said, sounding grim.

She trailed him to their horses, her steps heavy with foreboding, just as it began to snow. She could only hope they survived the night.

And that Cole would forgive her if they did.

Chapter 11

The snow fell steadily as the day wore on, building with the same relentless intensity as the certainty inside of Cole. If he'd needed proof that Bethany didn't belong in Maple Cove, Tony's accident had just provided it in spades.

He picked a trail through the snow-covered deadfall, then crossed a meadow in the deepening dusk. Seeing Bethany in action—her quick thinking under pressure, her obvious medical expertise—had forced him to view her in an altered light. And for the first time he understood why she'd needed to leave Maple Cove.

And why she could never stay.

Gunner stumbled on a patch of ice. "Whoa," Cole said, reining his exhausted horse to a halt. The frigid wind gusted, whipping pellets of snow at his face and bringing a chill scuttling over his skin. He turned up his collar and hunkered deeper into his saddle while he waited for Bethany to catch up.

She emerged from a cluster of trees a moment later, her black hat dusted with snowflakes, urging her tired mount up the treacherous slope. The muscles of his belly tightened, the inevitable surge of lust tempered with heavy guilt. It was bad enough that he'd exposed her to his father's attackers. Even worse, they were going to have one hell of a time driving those cows down the mountain through the snow. But all these years he'd misjudged her, blaming her for something that wasn't her fault—and he didn't like that one bit.

She came to a halt beside him, her nose pink from the bitter cold. "How much farther to the cattle?" she asked, her breath forming puffs in the air.

He twisted in his saddle and peered at the canyon ahead. "They're up that draw, near the divide."

"Can we make it there tonight?"

He shook his head, dislodging snow from the brim of his hat. "We'd better wait until daylight." He'd pushed the pace to make up the time they'd lost, but night was fast closing in. "The ride gets steeper from here on out, and I don't want to risk a fall."

"You want to camp here, then?"

He ran his gaze around the clearing. A stream gurgled nearby. Patches of grass still peeked through the blowing snow. A rocky overhang walled the northwest corner, offering some shelter from the blustery wind. "Yeah, this looks good."

"Great." She swung down from her horse, not quite managing to stifle a moan.

Wincing in sympathy, he dropped to the ground. "Sore?"

"Not too bad."

He didn't buy it. The strenuous ride had tired him out, and he spent every day on a horse. But Bethany rarely admitted to any weakness. She always suffered in stoic silence—a trait that both impressed and irritated him.

Like when she'd refused to reveal what had spooked her last night.

Too tired to summon any annoyance, he removed his gear from behind his saddle and hauled it to the rocks. "I'll take care of the horses if you set up camp and start a fire. But keep your rifle handy," he added.

"You think we're being followed?"

"No, but there's no point taking a chance."

He removed the saddles, then led the horses to the nearby creek, his thoughts still lingering on her. All this time he'd resented that she'd moved away, that she hadn't cared enough about him to stay. But there was nothing for her in Maple Cove. His expectations had been out of line.

And no matter how many grueling hours he'd spent in the saddle, no matter how relentless the pace he'd set, he couldn't outrun the truth. He hadn't been fair to her.

Not liking that blunt assessment, he hobbled the horses near their camp. Then he sat next to Bethany at the campfire and devoured a can of stew. But he could no longer deny the facts, no matter how unflattering they were. *He'd been wrong.*

Sobered by that brutal truth, he sat beside her in the flickering firelight, the welcome warmth heating his skin. His gaze kept returning to her high, sculpted cheekbones, her exotic, dark-lashed eyes. Her beauty made his heart thud. Every gesture, every graceful motion she made brought heat surging straight to his loins. And he had to admit that no matter what else had gone wrong between them, she still appealed to him in a basic, primal way.

And sitting together, snowflakes falling around them, the cold wind murmuring in the pines, it was far too easy to remember the good times, the reasons he'd once given her his heart—her intelligence, her patience, their easy camaraderie. She'd believed in his abilities. She'd encouraged him, given her unflagging support, and made him feel worthwhile.

But that was then. That time was gone. And in a few more days she'd once again exit his life. And he'd be on his ranch, just how he wanted to be.

Alone.

Pushing that thought aside with a frown, he finished his last can of stew. "You think Tony's all right?" he asked to distract himself.

She gave her head a quick shake. "It was a pretty bad break. He'll be out of commission for a while."

"Good. Then he'll have time to find a new job."

Her head came up. "You're not going to fire him?"

"Damn right I am." He didn't tolerate disrespect or disloyalty among his men.

"But…you can't. Your ranch hands just quit, and you need the help."

"I don't need it that bad." Hell, Tony was lucky he'd only escaped with a broken foot. Hearing him disparage Bethany had sent a bolt of white-hot rage blazing through him, incinerating his self-control. It had taken every ounce of willpower he had not to attack the injured man.

His belly hot with remembered anger, he surged to his feet, then returned his utensils to his pack.

Bethany rose and moved to his side. "Seriously, Cole. Don't be hasty. Wait until the problems with your father settle down before you make up your mind."

He shot her an incredulous look. "I can't believe you're defending him."

"I'm not. Not at all. I can't stand him. It's just—"

He stiffened. "None of my business?"

"No, that's not what I was going to say." The wind

gusted, making the pine trees creak. "It's just…complicated."

"It seems simple to me."

"I used to think so, too," she admitted. "The thing is… everyone pretends racism doesn't exist anymore. But it does. Not everyone is a racist by a long shot. There are lots of nice people around. But it happens, more than you'd expect."

"I know that." He'd felt the disapproval of some of the townspeople when he and Bethany had dated during high school. "But that doesn't mean I've got to tolerate it on my ranch."

"I don't expect you to. I'm just saying to wait for a better time before you fire him. Tony's a bully. He always has been. The racial aspects just give him another excuse to be mean. And maybe…maybe I misjudged him. My father says he does good work, so maybe you should give him another chance."

He doubted that. But her words triggered memories of the animosity he'd always sensed. And suddenly, it clicked. "Tony bullied you?"

She turned back toward the fire with a shrug. "When I was a kid."

"How?"

She kept her gaze on the flames. "The usual stuff— calling me names, pushing me around…"

And worse. He could hear the pain in her voice. He locked his jaw around a punch of anger. "You never told me that."

"There wasn't any point. He stopped once I learned to stand up for myself." She gave him a lopsided smile. "And when you and I started dating, he probably knew better than to risk your wrath."

"You got that right." He clenched his teeth, sudden

fury mixing with guilt. "I should have done something to stop it."

"I'm glad you didn't."

He raised a brow in surprise.

"It would have made me look weaker and encouraged him more."

"Maybe." All the same, Tony had a lot to answer for when they got back.

Bethany stepped even closer and laid her hand on his rigid arm. "There's nothing you could have done, Cole. I handled it myself."

"You shouldn't have had to." No wonder she acted so stoic. When had anyone stuck up for her?

He shook his head, appalled that he'd been so blind. How had he overlooked that meanness in Tony? How had he missed something so fundamental about her? First her need to leave, and now this. Had he been too wrapped up in the steamy sex to see who she really was?

Disgusted with himself, he let out a bitter laugh. "And I thought I knew you so well."

Her mouth quirked up. A deep, sensual heat flared in her eyes. "You knew me."

Their eyes locked. Awareness erupted between them, triggering the deep, prowling tension he'd battled to control for days.

He *knew* her, all right. He knew the hot, sultry taste of her skin, the sleek, moist heat of her lips. He knew her scent, her sighs, the whimper she made at the back of her throat, the dazed look in her pleasure-crazed eyes.

His heart began to pound. Blood pooled low in his groin. And memories flashed through his mind with brutal clarity—her ripe, pouting breasts, her nipples pebbling to invite his touch, the hot, tight feel of her pulsing around him, urging him to carnal bliss.

He reached out, fingered the ends of her long hair, the black silk igniting his nerves. He knew he shouldn't touch her. They had too much baggage between them. He had to step back, move away before he did something he'd regret.

But her lush lips parted. Her eyes turned luminous in the low light. He slid his hand along her jaw, her soft skin torching his hunger, and stroked his thumb down her silky throat.

"Cole," she whispered, the hoarse plea eroding his resolve.

Her pulse raced under his thumb. Her soft scent twined around him, trapping him in place. Unable to resist, he plunged his hands through her shiny hair, hauled her into his arms, and slanted his lips over hers.

Her potent mouth held him captive. The staggering feel of her overrode common sense. Warnings bleated through his mind, that this was wrong, senseless, that he would regret breaking his vow. Helpless to stop himself, he skimmed his hands down her shoulders and back, memorizing her contours with his hands. Then he tugged her tighter against him, the thrilling, feminine scent of her laying waste to what little remained of his self-control.

She moaned, and he delved deeper, his tongue mating with hers. Her round breasts pillowed his chest. Her lush hips cradled his. She was heaven, perfect, as enticing as he remembered. The answer to his erotic dreams.

And she kissed him back, her mewling sounds driving him crazy, her hands blazing a trail of lust through his nerves. She fueled a bone-deep craving inside him, torching a need he couldn't ignore.

Calling on all his remaining willpower, he managed to break off the kiss. He rested his forehead against hers, his breath sawing hard in the night. He wanted her under him, over him—any way he possibly could. He wanted to strip off her bulky clothes, expose her ripe, naked body to his gaze. And he wanted to lose himself deep inside her, taking her again and again until he was too damned sated to think.

But he had to stop. There were too many reasons this was wrong. And he was fast approaching the point of no return.

"Don't stop," she pleaded when he pulled back. Her kiss-swollen lips gleamed in the firelight. Her dark eyes burned into his. "Make love to me, Cole."

Heat stabbed his loins. His body turned rock-hard. "You're sure?" he made himself ask.

In answer, she stepped back and slipped off her sheepskin vest. She tugged her turtleneck over her head and stripped off her bra. His gaze fastened on her taut, high breasts, the flat, sleek line of her belly, the enticing indentation of her waist.

His jaw flexed. He made a low, rough growl in his throat. He couldn't think, suddenly couldn't remember why this was wrong. He could only watch her, riveted, as she steadily burned him alive.

The wind gusted. Her long, glossy hair slithered over her shoulders, framing her naked breasts. His pulse began to pound. A sweat broke out on his brow despite the frigid air. And he was lost. She called to something primitive inside him, needs he couldn't resist.

He kicked off his boots and peeled off his clothes, while she made short work of her own. Then she unzipped her sleeping bag, spread it over his, and slipped inside. He dove in after, his heart thundering, and pulled her soft feminine body under his.

His mouth descended on hers. A furious rush of wanting scalded his blood. He gave in to the demands bludgeoning his body, her wild urgency egging him on.

He finally broke the kiss, needing air. His pulse rocketing, he bracketed her face with his hands. And for a long moment he just drank in the sight of her—her dark, slumberous eyes, the delicate sweep of her cheeks. And emotions crowded in on him—yearning, lust, a feral feeling of possessiveness. She belonged right here in his arms.

He feathered kisses over her jaw, down the silky line of her throat, her soft moans filling the air. Then he moved lower, raking his teeth gently over her breasts. He took one sweet tip in his mouth, wringing a long, low groan from her throat. She gripped his hair and tugged him back up.

"Hurry," she urged, her eyes lost in desire. "I can't wait."

He nudged her legs apart with his knees. Then he fitted himself to her warmth, the scent of her provoking a riot of lust in his blood.

She'd given him her virginity. He'd claimed her that day long ago, branding her as his own. She'd surrendered to him, giving herself with an intimacy that went far beyond sex, beyond the mating of their bodies, to a fundamental need.

He entered her in a desperate thrust, the tight, velvet feel of her igniting a savagery inside him, the pleasure so staggering he growled. She was hot, moist, perfect. Everything he'd ever wanted.

And she was his.

She began to move against him. He took her mouth again in a hot, frenzied kiss that obliterated every thought. His heart thudded hard. Hot blood thrummed through his veins. He sank into her welcoming heat, his body picking up the ancient rhythm, needing her in a way he couldn't explain.

"Bethany," he groaned, his breathing labored.

He felt her tighten around him. Her muscles bore down, her eyes turning crazed, and then she let out a keening cry.

He couldn't stop. Completely at his body's mercy, he made one final thrust, then exploded, a hoarse shout wrenched from his lungs.

For an eternity he didn't move, the pleasure still pumping through him, his breath ragged in the quiet night. Then he kissed her, long and hard and deep, expressing everything he couldn't say. Tenderness. Admiration. Desire.

He knew he should feel guilty. He'd had no business making love to Bethany when so much between them was wrong. But it was hard to summon regrets when it felt so incredibly right.

He buried his face in her hair, the tremors slowly ebbing from his body, her warm breath fanning his ear. Wrong or not, he doubted he'd ever get enough of her. She suited him in too many ways to count.

But the world-shattering sex changed nothing. She wouldn't stay. She belonged in Chicago where she could make good use of her skills. And he could never go.

Worrying that his weight would crush her, he rolled over, taking her with him, and settled her on top. Then he dragged the sleeping bag over her naked back, protecting her from the encroaching cold.

And for a moment, he acknowledged the longing hovering at the edge of his heart, the desire to hold her forever in his arms. But that was dangerous ground to tread, a place he could never go. He had to keep his emotional distance, just as he'd vowed at the start. He couldn't fight her battles, couldn't let himself get involved too deeply and begin to care.

But as she nibbled kisses down his unshaven jaw, sparking another savage rush of desire, he feared that he'd never stopped.

* * *

Bethany awoke near dawn, cocooned in glorious heat. Cole lay on his side behind her, his heavy arm draped over her hip, his hard muscles warming her back. Her limbs felt deliciously languid, her body so limp with pleasure she could hardly hold on to a thought.

Except one. She'd made a reckless mistake. Making love with Cole hadn't solved any problems; it had only made her dilemma worse. She still hadn't told him about the man who'd tried to kill her. She hadn't revealed that her father might be harboring secrets about the ranch.

But exactly what could she tell him? Tony's fierce denial had destroyed her leading theory, throwing her beliefs in disarray. But she knew one thing. If her father *did* have any role in this, *he* should come clean and confess it. She'd already misjudged Tony, letting her resentment over his harassment cloud her mind. She couldn't falsely accuse her father, too.

But what about Cole? He deserved to know the truth. And if he found out later that she'd deceived him…

His hand moved to her breast, the rough calluses teasing her nerves, and she instinctively arched her back. He brushed aside her hair, slid his mouth down the nape of her neck, the sexy rasp of his beard stubble making her sigh.

Wrong or not, she couldn't resist him. Everything about this man appealed to her—the hard, rugged planes of his face, his utterly carnal kiss, the devastating thoroughness with which he made love. He detonated her senses, taking her to heights she'd never imagined, until he'd reduced her to wanting to beg.

But she couldn't ignore the irony. The man who electrified her nerves—the only man she'd ever loved—was exactly the one she could never have.

His hand slipped between her legs. Pleasure coiled inside her, the feel so exquisite on her sensitized skin she nearly climaxed at once.

But instead of continuing, he went still. She arched against him, already lost to sensations, her body moistening for his.

But he didn't move. "Shhh," he hissed, his urgent tone penetrating the fog of desire. "We've got company."

She froze, the torrid feelings shattered. Her heart catapulted against her rib cage; her senses went fully alert. She skipped her gaze around the shadowed clearing, the trees barely visible in the predawn light. The horses stamped their hooves. Taut silence pulsed in the air.

And fear turned her belly to ice.

How could she have let her guard down? How could she have forgotten, even for a moment, that they had a killer on their heels? And why hadn't she warned Cole about that truck?

Cole soundlessly began tugging on clothes. She did the same, her throat bone-dry, her hands trembling as she snapped her jeans.

She reached for her rifle next to the bedroll.

Just as all hell broke loose.

Chapter 12

Gunfire erupted around them. A bullet ricocheted off the rocky overhang, shearing chips of stone onto their heads. Bethany lunged for her .22 and racked a round as Cole got off a shot toward the trees.

"Get behind the boulder," he urged, still firing.

Not unless he went with her. Her pulse running wild, Bethany sighted down the barrel of her rifle and pumped a shot at the pines. Cole rolled to his feet and hauled her upright as more gunfire came from the woods. They dove for cover behind the rock.

The shooting paused. Her heartbeat frenzied, Bethany struggled to catch her breath.

Cole reloaded his weapon, his furious eyes flashing at her. "Why didn't you run?"

"I was trying to protect you."

"By nearly getting killed?"

Not bothering to answer, she chambered a round in her rifle, then peeked from behind the rock. The horses had moved to the edge of the clearing. The trees swayed in the low dawn light. The cold wind gusted, whipping up embers from their campfire and making the pine boughs creak.

"How many shooters are there?" she asked, keeping her voice low.

His jaw like granite, he shot her another scowl. "Two, I think. I'm going to circle around and check. Stay here and cover for me."

"But—"

"I mean it, Bethany." His eyes sparked at hers. "Stay behind this rock. Just keep on firing until I get into the woods."

He rose to a crouch. She stood at the edge of the boulder and aimed her gun toward the trees.

"Now!"

Steeling her nerves, she started firing. Cole sprinted full out toward the horses, then melted into the woods. Once she was certain he'd made it, she ducked behind the rock.

An ominous stillness again descended. Her heart jackhammered in her throat. Where were their attackers? Why hadn't they shot back? What if they'd ambushed Cole?

Trying not to imagine the worst, she checked the rounds in her gun. Only two left. She hesitated, then slid her gaze to the saddle bag she'd left by the campfire—containing her extra shells. She hated to leave the safety of the rock, but running out of ammunition could get them killed.

She inhaled and gathered her courage, preparing to dart over and grab the bag. But then a movement in the clearing caught her eye.

She whipped around. A man rushed toward her—his pistol raised. Her heart rocketing, she pumped off a shot at his arm.

He reeled around and staggered backward, then

stumbled back into the trees. Her hands trembling, she ejected the spent shell and racked her final round. She didn't want to kill a man, no matter what his intentions toward her.

But she might not have a choice.

Not wanting to think about that dizzying prospect, she dragged in a shaky breath. Then she shifted her attention to her bag. She had to get those extra shells *now*.

She sprinted toward the campfire. Shots rang out, hitting the rock face behind her, and she zigzagged to the bag. She scooped it up, skidded back to the boulder, then scrambled behind it again. She hit the ground and gasped for breath.

She was safe—for now. But where was Cole? What was he doing? Had any of those shots been aimed at him?

That thought threatened to unnerve her, but she ruthlessly pushed it aside. Cole couldn't be hurt. She refused even to think it. No matter what else happened, he had to survive.

Still trembling, she fumbled in her bag for the box of shells. Then she loaded the magazine on her rifle and settled in to wait for Cole.

Seconds ticked past. The wind howled in the trees. She debated going after Cole, but forced herself to stay put. But she couldn't stem the torrent of guilt. She should have told Cole about her father. She never should have lied about that truck. She'd had no right to keep the truth from him. *He could have died.*

A twig snapped nearby. Her heart racing, she raised her gun and aimed.

"It's me," Cole called out. "I'm coming in."

She inched out her breath, but kept her rifle trained on the trees to guard against any tricks. But Cole emerged from the forest alone, and she finally lowered her gun.

He strode across the clearing. His eyes connected with hers, and he came to a sudden halt. "What happened?" He rushed the final distance between them. "You're bleeding."

Bleeding? She pressed her hand to her temple. Her fingers came away sticky. And suddenly, she was aware of the moisture trickling down her jaw, the dull throb in her scalp.

He gently lifted her chin, angling his head to see. "They shot you."

"No. I don't think so." Surely she would have felt more pain. "A piece of rock must have splintered off and hit me when I ran over to get more shells."

His hand stilled. His eyes cut to hers. "You did what?"

"I needed more ammunition. I was nearly out. So I ran over to get my bag."

His jaw worked. A muscle ticked in his cheek. Then he moved his face even closer, his eyes blazing at hers. "I told you not to move. Do you have a death wish?"

"I didn't have much choice."

"The hell you didn't. You could have died."

"So could you." Their eyes dueled. She let out a heavy sigh. "It's just a scrape, Cole. Nothing major. I'll bandage it when we've got time."

His jaw still rigid, he looked away. She could tell he was fighting his emotions, trying to keep his temper under control. But she didn't need him to worry about her.

"Did you see who was out there?" she asked.

He gave a curt nod. "Two men on horseback. No one I recognized. There might have been a third farther off. They're heading downhill right now, but they could circle back."

"I shot one in the arm." She started to tell him the details, but his furious gaze stopped her cold. Better that he didn't know how close the man had come. "But it might not hold them off for long," she added.

His mouth turned even grimmer, forming brackets in his unshaven jaw. "We'd better head out before they come back."

"Right." She hesitated. "Cole, listen. About the other night, when I went to the library in Bozeman—"

"We'll talk later. We need to get moving."

He was right. There wasn't time for explanations with the killers lurking nearby. But before this ordeal was over, she had to reveal what she knew. She couldn't withhold the truth with their lives at risk.

While Cole hurried to saddle the horses, she doused what remained of the campfire and threw together their gear. Then she sprang up on Red, keeping her .22 within reach in the scabbard, and took off with Cole up the draw.

But as they worked their way up the icy slope, night giving way to a somber dawn, the extent of their predicament sank in. The killers knew where they were now. They had no way to call for help. And once they found the cattle, they had to head back down the mountain—possibly into an ambush.

And she only had herself to blame.

They trudged through the mountains for miles, the arctic wind bearing down with a vengeance, whipping the snow sideways and reducing the visibility to nil. Shivering, Bethany pulled her wool scarf higher over her nose and hunched her shoulders in the frosty air. But even the bitter cold penetrating her bones couldn't distract her from her mounting guilt.

She'd screwed up terribly during her time in Maple Cove. She'd done an injustice to Tony. She'd failed to confront her father and lied to Cole. And instead of coming clean and warning Cole about the threats, she'd recklessly indulged in a night of passion, nearly getting them killed.

The snow swirled, and she caught a glimpse of him on his horse—his broad back straight, his head swiveling as he surveyed the terrain—and her heart made a heavy lurch. Of all the things she'd done wrong, making love with Cole had been the worst—and not only because of the danger they were in.

It had stirred up too many memories, making her yearn for things she couldn't have.

But no matter how thrilling his touch, no matter how amazing the feel of him, what they'd shared wasn't real. It had been a moment out of time, a magical interlude. And the last thing she needed was an excuse to start fantasizing about him. She was already perilously close to falling in love with him again.

She caught her breath, horrified at the thought. *No way.* She absolutely could not fall in love with Cole. So what if he embodied her dreams? So what if she admired the man he'd become? They had no future together. And she'd spent enough time grieving his loss the first time. She refused to go through that torture again—no matter who'd been at fault.

Cole pulled Gunner to a stop. She straggled to a halt beside him, struggling to harness her traitorous thoughts. But then she dragged her gaze to where he was looking. Dark-red splashes dotted the snow.

Blood.

Her breath stopped. She pulled her rifle from her scabbard, her senses suddenly alert.

"Stay behind me," Cole said, urging his horse forward.

Her heart beating fast, she fell in behind him as he threaded his way through the trees. The trail of blood continued. The bitter wind thrashed the pines. They rode for dozens of yards, the bloodstains growing bigger. Then, by the edge of a tiny clearing, tufts of fur stood out in the snow—the remains of a Black Angus calf.

Her stomach tumbled. Cole leaped down, his horse shying from the scent of blood. Bethany leaned over and grabbed Gunner's reins while Cole inspected the calf.

"What do you think? Coyotes?" she asked, a heavy feeling settling inside her at the thought of the helpless calf.

He walked around the carcass, pausing to study the tracks. "Wolves, judging by the claw marks."

"Wolves?" She frowned at that. There were a couple known wolf packs in the area, but they normally left the livestock alone.

"Either way, they haven't gone far," Cole said. "The kill is fresh."

His eyes troubled, he came back and took Gunner's reins. Then he swung himself into the saddle and rode off, following the churned-up snow.

Her own misgivings growing, she clucked Red into motion and trailed him up the slope. Poor Cole. He definitely didn't need more trouble. That secret society had shot his cattle. They'd killed a man, burned his barn, and tried to murder him. And if that weren't enough to deal with, he now had to contend with wolves.

And this was partly her fault. She'd contributed to this mess indirectly, allowing those men to get close. Which meant she had to help fix it. But how?

The sound of lowing cattle reached her ears. Cole nudged Gunner into a trot, and Bethany followed, the freezing wind lashing her face. She crested a rise, then spotted the herd below them in a meadow ringed with towering pines. The cattle were huddled together, indicating that the predators weren't far off.

"You think they're all here?" she asked Cole.

"I hope so. I'll try to get a count. Wait here and make sure they don't take off." He reined Gunner around and rode up the side of the herd.

Bethany sipped some water from her canteen, the half-frozen liquid making her molars ache, then scanned the rugged terrain. Dense stands of timber covered the mountains below the tree line. At higher elevations, granite outcrops jutted from the mounting snow. Gunmetal clouds inched across the range, their wispy edges obscuring the highest peaks.

The wolves were their immediate problem, along with the deadly cold. But assuming they survived those issues, they still had to deal with those killers, who'd be lying in wait below. And there wasn't another route down the mountain.

Unless they went over the pass...

Her pulse quickened. She peered through the blowing snow, wracking her memory for details of the terrain. From what she remembered, it wouldn't be easy. The slope was steep, treacherous, especially in the snow. They'd have to cross various streams, making it hard to manage the herd. But if they succeeded, they could escape those men.

And just maybe, she could make up for the harm she'd done.

But first she had to convince Cole.

He rode back a minute later, snowflakes covering his wide shoulders, his face swarthy from the cold. Her traitorous heart faltered when his gaze landed on hers. She wondered wildly if she could ever react normally to this man.

"They're all here," he said. "It looks like we only lost that one calf."

"That's a relief." Although she still felt bad for the calf.

"Yeah." He angled his stubble-roughened jaw toward

the trail. "We'd better start down while we've still got light. We'll set up camp when it gets dark."

"I have a better idea. Let's go across the divide." He opened his mouth to argue, and she forged on. "It's a risk, I know. But it would shorten the distance a lot. And once we get near the highway we can pick up a signal on our cell phones and call for help."

"It's not just risky, it's suicidal."

"So is riding into an ambush. You know those men are going to come back."

"But at least this way we have a chance." He shook his head. "We're tired. The horses are nearly done in. We can't keep pushing them all night. And that storm's about to pick up. It could dump a couple of feet of snow before daylight, closing off that pass."

"All the more reason to try it. You know those men won't expect it. They'll be waiting for us to go back the way we came."

"Because it's the only way we *can* go."

"No, it's not. We can make it across that pass."

His mouth flattened. "I'm not willing to take the chance."

"But why not?" He had to know it made sense. And he wasn't the type to quail before a challenge, especially if it would save his herd.

She frowned at him in frustration. They would run into an ambush down the trail. He knew that as well as she did.

Unless he planned to sacrifice his cattle to get her through.

Horror rippled through her. She stared at him, aghast. But she knew instantly that she was right. He'd protected the father who'd treated him badly. He planned to fire Tony for insulting her, even though it hurt his ranch. And now he was willing to risk himself—and the future of his beloved ranch—to make sure she survived.

And suddenly, she realized she wasn't close to falling in love with Cole, she'd already taken the plunge.

He exhaled. "Look, Bethany. You're exhausted. We both are. Let's head down the trail a ways and make camp. We'll deal with the danger in the morning."

Badly shaken by the revelation, she looked away. She was tempted to agree. Her body ached. She could hardly feel her frozen toes. And the thought of going over that pass in the darkness, the cold wind howling around them, didn't appeal to her in the least. They could get frostbitten or attacked by predators, lose their footing and stumble over a cliff. And she needed time to compose herself, to sort through her emotions and gather her defenses against Cole.

But she'd damaged him enough. She'd hurt him badly when she'd left after high school, reinforcing his lack of trust. Maybe she could never repair that. She couldn't undo the past. But she could save the one thing he cared about—his ranch.

She stuffed her rifle back into the scabbard and tightened her grip on Red's reins. And a deep feeling of certainty settled inside her. *This was right.*

She wheeled her horse around, then glanced back and met Cole's eyes. "Suicidal or not, I'm taking the cattle over that pass."

Then, with the snow whipping against her, she started to ride.

Cole didn't know which he wanted to do more—strangle Bethany or hole up in a cave somewhere and make love to her for days.

He picked his way down the icy hill in the predawn

darkness, riding ahead of the exhausted herd. He still couldn't believe she'd insisted on taking this treacherous route, risking her life to save his cows. He'd never been more in awe of her courage and determination.

Or more scared.

The wind gusted sideways, pelting Cole with ice. His back ached; his face was frozen stiff. His stomach had gone beyond empty the day before. Even his horse could barely stay upright, plodding wearily through the snow.

He brought his worn-out horse to a halt and glanced back at the lowing herd. Incredibly, they'd navigated the slippery slopes without a mishap—thanks to Bethany's skill. And he couldn't believe her stamina. They'd spent twenty hours straight in the saddle, and she still kept slogging on.

But at long last they'd nearly reached the road. As soon as he could get a signal bar on his cell phone, he'd call for trucks to pick up the cattle and get the sheriff to deal with those men.

And then he'd get as far from Bethany as he could. He desperately needed space to regain his equilibrium and get his mind off the torrid sex. Because if he didn't come to his senses soon he'd do something he'd regret.

Like beg her to stay.

Without warning, Gunner balked. Snapping his attention back to his horse, Cole reined him hard to the right. But Gunner only pranced sideways, trying to distance himself from the trees.

Alert now, Cole scanned the forest for signs of danger. Gunner tossed up his head and snorted, sensing something Cole couldn't see. The cows continued plodding past him, funneling into a valley flanked by the timbered hills.

Bethany rode up a minute later, her eyes exhausted, the

wool scarf she'd wrapped around her face crusted with snow. "What's wrong?" she asked, her voice muffled.

"Nothing yet, but Gunner's acting spooked."

"You think the wolves are still nearby?"

"Something is." He returned his gaze to the timber, and uneasiness crawled through his nerves. "Take the lead. I'll bring up the rear." Wolves would be more likely to attack a faltering cow. "Turn the herd when the valley levels out. If you go straight you'll go over a cliff."

"All right." She nudged Red forward.

"And Bethany?" She halted Red and looked back. "Be careful."

Their eyes held. Emotions swirled inside him, a jumble of feelings he didn't care to name. She nodded, then rode up the line.

Still beating back his tumultuous feelings, Cole waited for the rest of the herd to pass by, his eyes on a trio of dawdling cows. Reining in Gunner with effort, he circled behind the stragglers to hurry them back into the herd.

But Gunner ignored his command and spun around. Cole hauled on the reins, battling to control his panicked horse. "Whoa," he said. "What the…"

And then he saw them, their eyes glowing, creeping silently from the woods.

Wolves.

His heart stopped. Still fighting his spinning horse, he grabbed his rifle from the scabbard and racked a round. The wolves began to spread out, acting on some hidden signal, forming a semicircle around the frightened cows.

Using all his strength, Cole forced his spooked horse backward, trying to stay between the wolves and the vulnerable cows. But a huge black wolf stalked forward. He paced back and forth, steadily coming closer, then stopped and began to howl.

The others joined in. The eerie sound sent a chill jolting down Cole's spine. Gunner rolled his eyes and tried to run, but Cole managed to hold him in place. He couldn't abandon his cows.

The lead wolf yipped. The wolves began to move. Cole continued riding backward, praying Bethany stayed away. He didn't want her trying something heroic that could get her killed.

The leader growled, his hackles rising, his wild eyes fixed on Cole. Cole's fingers twitched, but he held his fire. He couldn't legally shoot the endangered wolves unless they attacked him first.

Suddenly Bethany came racing toward him, and his stomach coiled with dread. "Get back," he shouted. "For God's sake, get away."

Ignoring him, she pressed forward. She pulled to a stop beside him, then fired a warning shot in the air.

The wolves turned toward her, their attention snagged. And then the lead wolf charged.

Chapter 13

Cole didn't hesitate. He fired at the wolf just as Bethany's gun barked out. The animal stumbled, then dropped in its tracks.

The other wolves paused. Behind him, the panicked cows scattered, racing down the valley toward the herd. His heart galloping, Cole hauled on the reins, battling to keep Gunner from bolting after the cows. A flight response would trigger another attack.

He kept his gaze on the ring of wolves. Their savage eyes gleamed back. "Don't move," he warned Bethany.

"I'm trying not to," she gritted out, struggling to control her frantic horse.

He rose in the stirrups and waved his gun at the wolves. "Go on. Get out of here!" Several turned tail and slunk back into the woods.

Encouraged, he fired a shot in the air. "Get out. Go!" he shouted again, and the last few wolves disappeared.

His eyes still locked on the forest, Cole hissed his breath through his teeth. That had been too damned close.

He waited several heartbeats to make sure they wouldn't come back. Then he reined Gunner around, giving vent to his gut-wrenching fear. "What the hell were you thinking? I told you to stay away. Those wolves could have—"

A deep drumming sound snagged his attention. He snapped his gaze to the valley and peered through the shadowy snow. Bethany shoved her rifle into the scabbard and urged Red forward just as he registered what was wrong.

Stampede.

His heart stumbled hard. Fierce dread shot through his veins. The cows were running through a valley. At the end was a cliff. If the herd didn't turn in time...

And Bethany had just leaped into the melée.

He kicked Gunner into action, then charged down the snowy slope after Bethany, pushing his horse to a breakneck pace. He had to get Bethany out of there before they reached that cliff.

"Bethany!" he shouted, but the bellowing of the herd, the thundering of hoofbeats drowned him out.

Fueled by abject panic, he dug his heels into Gunner, accelerating to a reckless speed. The bitter wind whipped past. The horse skidded, but regained his feet. Cole squinted, riding like a fury, trying to see Bethany in the blinding snow.

"Come on. Come on," he urged Gunner. He hurtled down the icy valley, leaping over rocks and deadfall, terror lodged tight in his throat. Then he drove his exhausted horse even harder. He knew he was risking a deadly crash but didn't have a choice.

After a moment he saw her, riding near the edge of the panicked herd. He knew what she intended. She'd try to outrun the cows and turn them, curving them inward to end the stampede.

But if she failed…

His heart congealed. A wild feeling of dread seized his gut. Forcing Gunner to the absolute limit, he raced alongside the herd, slowly gaining ground on Bethany as they neared the cliff. But they would never make it. They were running out of time.

She miraculously gained the lead. The valley leveled out—and his heart stopped dead. Only a few more yards to the cliff.

But she pulled out her rifle and fired into the air. The lead cows balked and turned away. She held her ground, still shooting above their heads, and the column began to curve. Cole reached her side a second later, and added his shouts and shots to hers.

The startled cows slowed. They gradually began to mill around, their frenzied flight finally subdued. Cole let out an incredulous breath, amazed that Bethany had pulled it off.

But she had nearly died.

He pulled his blowing horse to a stop. He leaped down and stormed through the snow, then pulled her off her horse.

Her full mouth wobbled. Her eyes were huge in her pale face. Her courage and fragility slammed through him, a sucker punch to his heart.

Overwhelmed by a barrage of emotions, he hauled her into his arms. He closed his eyes, buried his face in her silky hair, and then just held her, his heart beating violently, relief shuddering through him, his feelings a disordered mess. She'd risked her life to save his stampeding cattle. She'd endangered herself to fight those wolves.

He'd never met anyone so brave or reckless or amazing in his life.

He lifted his head, raised his hands to her delicate jaw, framing her ashen face with his hands. He gazed into her glimmering eyes, still unable to form a word. Then he bent and fitted his mouth to hers, glorying in the soft, living feel of her, giving vent to his terror, his awe.

His love.

His heart tumbled hard. He pressed her tighter against him, buffeted by his raging emotions, pouring everything into the kiss—everything he couldn't say. Revealing his fear, his yearning, his need.

He'd nearly lost her. That horrific thought kept ricocheting through his mind, threatening to drive him insane. He plundered her lips, her mouth, needing to convince himself she was alive.

With effort, he ended the kiss and tucked her head against his neck. For an eternity he continued to hold her, stunned by the feelings churning inside him, absorbing the wonder of her safe in his arms.

Words bubbled up, but he steeled his jaw to keep them from breaking free. No matter how desperately he wanted this woman, he couldn't go through this again. She was going to leave. He had no right to ask her to stay. He couldn't put his heart on the line.

Still badly shaken, he filled his lungs with the frosty air, then forced himself to pull back. "Are you all right?" he asked, his voice rough.

"I'm fine. Now." She managed a crooked smile, but he saw how shaken she was. "Just exhausted and anxious to get home," she added.

Home. Chicago. The place where she belonged.

He took another step back. "We're almost to the road. We might be able to get a signal on our cell phones now."

Still struggling to control his emotions, he turned away and mounted his weary horse. She'd exposed feelings he'd stifled for years, longings he shouldn't have—no matter how right she felt in his arms.

Tossed thoroughly off balance, he waited until she'd mounted Red, then started herding the weary cattle toward the road. But as they plodded along, he had to face the truth.

He loved her. He always would.

And there wasn't a damned thing he could do about it, except to protect himself the only way he knew how—by shutting down.

Bethany awoke from an exhausted slumber hours later. She opened her eyes, disoriented, and blinked at the fresh patches of snow dotting the gravel road. She glanced out the window, recognized the old stagecoach stop on a distant hill. They'd nearly reached Cole's ranch.

She turned her attention to "Rocky" Rockwell, the deputy sheriff driving the SUV, and the past few hours rushed back. They'd loaded up the horses and cattle. They'd reported the wolf attack to the feds. Cole had hustled her into the deputy's SUV, turning the heater on full blast, then talked to the sheriff about the men. She'd fallen asleep the minute she hit the seat.

She spotted Cole's truck ahead and sighed, missing him already, but knew the separation would do her good. She'd been far too tempted to blurt out that she loved him— which wouldn't have been fair to him. They had no chance for a future until she revealed the truth.

And maybe not even then. Assuming he forgave her deception, even if he wanted to share her future, where would they live? He'd never leave his ranch and move to Chicago, and she still couldn't stay here.

But first things first. As soon as they arrived at the ranch she had to tell him about the attack in Bozeman and apologize for endangering his life. She also had to get answers from her father, confess that she'd suspected him all along—and hope Cole understood.

They hit a section of washboard, and the SUV rattled as hard as her jittering nerves. Then they crested a rise outside the ranch. Dozens of trucks and cars crowded the gravel road, taking her by surprise.

"What's going on?" People congregated in the neighbor's field. A television van recorded the scene. More people toting cameras surrounded the wooden gate.

The deputy grimaced. "Word of Lana's kidnapping leaked out and the media is going nuts."

"Oh, no." The blitz surrounding the senator's infidelities had been bad enough. This would feed the media frenzy and fuel the tabloids for weeks—causing headaches Cole didn't need.

The deputy slowed as they neared the crowd, catching up to Cole. Journalists swarmed both vehicles, flashing cameras and hurling questions their way. "Idiots," Rocky muttered. "Trying to get run over." He honked and inched toward the gate.

Minutes later, they made it through. The reporters hung back, unable to trespass on private land. Bethany exhaled, relieved to finally escape the frantic crowd.

But now she had an even bigger hurdle to face.

The deputy parked beside the machinery shed, alongside Cole. Bethany climbed out, her muscles stiff, her head still dizzy with fatigue. But she'd sleep more later. She had to make a confession first.

Her heart beating triple-time, she went in search of Cole. She found him beside the machinery shed, talking to Earl. "Can I help?" she asked, glancing around.

His eyes met hers, triggering the usual sensual jolt. "No. Earl's taking care of the horses. Go grab something to eat. We need to give the sheriff a statement as soon as he shows up."

"All right." She hesitated, her belly fluttering. "But if you have a minute, I need to talk to you…alone."

"Sure."

She waited while Cole wrapped things up with Earl, her tension rising with every second that passed. Why had she waited so long to tell him? How could she possibly explain?

They began walking toward the ranch house. She sneaked a glance at his rough-hewn profile, experiencing another attack of nerves.

"So what did you want to say?" he asked.

She inhaled. There was no good way to say it. She had to blurt it out. "I, um… I didn't tell you, but that day I went to Bozeman to do research at the library someone tried to run me off the road."

He abruptly came to a halt. "What?"

She hugged her arms, but couldn't stem the anxiety welling inside. "On the way home that night there was a truck. I couldn't see who it was. He had his bright lights on… He hit my bumper and tried to force me off the road."

"And you didn't tell me?"

"I should have, I know. But I thought…" She dragged in another breath. "You wouldn't let me go to the mountains if you knew."

He gaped at her, incredulity in his eyes. "And that mattered?"

"Yes. I thought Tony was causing the problems on the ranch. It was my only chance to confront him. But I was wrong. I made a mistake. I let my feelings about him cloud my judgment. And as a result…I put us all at risk."

His eyes stayed on hers. Several heartbeats passed. Then he tore his gaze away and stared into the distance, as if grappling for something to say.

"You lied to me." His voice sounded dead.

Her stomach swooped. "I… Yes, I did." She searched for a way to explain. But she had betrayed his trust. How could she rationalize that?

"Cole, I…"

The sheriff's deputy sauntered over, his boots crunching on the gravel drive. "Sheriff Colton's almost here," he said. "He said to tell you he'll need a statement from you both."

Cole nodded and glanced his way. "We'll wait in the house." His eyes cut back to hers. The coldness in them froze her heart.

And the terrible realization slammed through her. He wouldn't forgive her deception.

And he hadn't even heard the worst.

Bethany huddled in an armchair a short time later, nursing a hot cup of tea. Despite a scalding shower, an afghan wrapped around her shoulders and her thickest pair of wool socks, she still couldn't seem to warm up. Cole hadn't looked at her since she'd sat down.

"How about you, Bethany?" the sheriff asked, drawing her reluctant attention to him. "Do you have anything to add to Cole's report?"

"Not that I can think of." She'd told him about the truck. She'd described the man she'd shot. "I only saw the one man."

The sheriff snapped his notebook closed. "I've put out an alert. If he goes anywhere for medical treatment, we'll pick him up." He paused, then glanced around the group. "If there's nothing else, I'll head back to town."

Her stomach like lead, Bethany looked at her father. He sat across from her on the couch, his wrinkled face pasty, his gnarled hands tightly clasped.

Why didn't he speak out?

The sheriff stood. Dread settled around her heart. And she knew she had to act. She hated to confront her father in public, but she had to reveal the truth.

"Wait," she said. The sheriff turned back. Everyone looked her way.

Swallowing hard, she met her father's eyes. "Dad?" she whispered. "You know something, don't you?"

He opened his mouth, as if to protest. "Dad, please," she pleaded. "We really need to know."

He hesitated, then seemed to deflate. He slumped back against the cushions, his face even more waxy, looking every one of his sixty-eight years.

"You're right. I…I do have something to say," he admitted. "Something I should have said a long time ago. I know who's involved in this."

The sheriff sat back down. Bethany braved a glance at Cole, who sat with deceptive stillness, his arms crossed, his eyes riveted on her dad. Her hopes plummeted. He was furious. She should never have concealed the truth.

Her father let out a breath. "You were right that someone at the ranch was involved. It's Kenny Greene."

"Kenny?" she repeated, stunned. The mild-mannered boy she'd gone to school with? The boy Tony had bullied along with her? "But why?"

"Money. I guess he wanted to buy that fancy rig."

"You'd better start at the beginning," the sheriff said, sounding grim.

Her father nodded, but dropped his gaze to his hands. "The day I got hurt, I was riding in the pasture by the teepee ring. I saw Kenny with some men I didn't know. I went to find out what they were doing on the ranch.

"They were going to shoot me. For what it's worth, Kenny convinced them I wouldn't talk. They tied me to the stirrup, made Red drag me a ways. After my leg broke, they cut me loose."

Bethany closed her eyes, not wanting to imagine the horror, the humiliation and pain.

"They told me if I kept my mouth shut no one else would get hurt." He lifted his gaze to Cole. "I didn't know about your sister, the kidnapping. I thought they would cut some fences, maybe break another window, and you'd make the senator leave."

"And when they killed that mercenary?" Cole asked, his voice so icy it made her heart lurch. "Why the hell didn't you say something then?"

"I wanted to, but Kenny cornered me the day before. He said they'd kill Bethany if I talked."

Her mind flashed back to the day they'd brought the cows in, when she'd seen them beside the corral. She'd attributed his pallor to his injury, not fear.

"They'd already broken my leg. I knew they'd follow through with their threat. But now..." His voice dropped. "It's gone too far."

Dead silence gripped the room. Her heart wrenched for her father, even as her anger rose. The man she'd idolized all her life, the man she'd revered, had let her down.

But he'd kept silent to protect her. Hadn't she done the same for him? They'd both acted badly.

And as a result, they'd hurt Cole.

She looked at Cole. His jaw was bunched, his eyes cold. And panic spurted inside her. Somehow she had to convince him of their good intentions. Somehow she had to explain.

"Can you describe the men who hurt you?" the sheriff asked.

Her father nodded. "Yeah. I'm pretty good with faces."

"Good." The sheriff stood. "Be at the station at four. I'll call in an artist from Bozeman so we can start circulating some pictures of these guys." He turned to Cole. "I'll put out an APB for Kenny, but he's probably skipped town."

Suddenly remembering the bridle piece in her pocket, Bethany rose and fished it out. "I found this in the field. I don't know if it means anything." She handed it to him.

"I'll check it out. Maybe we'll get lucky and find a match. God knows we can use a break." The sheriff and his deputy went to the door. Cole let them out, and their footsteps slowly faded. A hush fell over the room.

Her father grabbed his crutches, then hobbled over to Cole, who still stood near the door. "Cole, I'm sorry. I thought…" He hung his head. "Hell, there's no excuse. It was a damned fool thing to do. I'll pack my bag and go."

His shoulders slumped, looking thoroughly defeated, her father limped toward his room. She watched him go, aching to console him.

But first she had to talk to Cole.

Swallowing hard, she started toward Cole. But he stalked to his study and slammed the door, the harsh finality of the sound giving rise to another swarm of nerves.

Pausing, she met Hannah's eyes. The housekeeper stood by the kitchen, a stricken expression on her face. "He just needs time. He—he's had a lot of disappointments in his life."

Bethany managed to nod. But Hannah was wrong. If she didn't reach Cole now, she never would.

Her heart pounding, she went to the study door. She raised her hand to knock, then reconsidered. She twisted the knob and went in.

Cole stood by the window, staring out at the burned barn. "Cole?" she whispered.

His back stiffened. "Go away."

"I—I'd like to explain."

"I don't want to hear it."

"I know that, but I have to tell you—"

He whipped around. His furious eyes slashed at hers. "Fine. You want to explain why you covered up for your father? Go right ahead."

Her stomach balled. "I didn't cover up exactly. I didn't know anything for sure."

"But you suspected. My cattle were dying. Men were getting killed. Hell, my sister was being held prisoner—and you didn't say a word."

"It wasn't that simple."

"The hell it wasn't.

"It wasn't. I wanted to tell you. I really did. But I didn't have anything to go on. And I couldn't accuse my dad without proof.

"You don't know what it's like," she continued. "All my life people have misjudged me. They see the color of my skin and assume all sorts of things—that I'm lazy, that I steal. Even in Chicago, where I thought my coworkers knew me, they've accused me of something I didn't do. And I couldn't do that to my father. Not without proof."

She drew in a ragged breath. "He's my father, Cole, the only family I have. I owed him at least that much."

"So you lied."

"I was wrong," she admitted. "I know that now. But you've made mistakes. You've done things that you regret."

He let out a bitter sound. "I've made mistakes, all right."

He meant her.

Her face burned. A huge ache constricted her chest. "Cole…"

"Your father's leaving," he continued, his voice hard. "I want you out of here, too."

Sudden panic gripped her. She had to reach him. *He had to understand.* "Don't do this," she pleaded. "Don't shut me out again. Can't we talk—"

"Get out, Bethany. You've done enough damage. Go back to Chicago where you belong."

Her throat closed tight. A huge wave of despair swamped her heart. He wouldn't forgive her. He wouldn't give her another chance.

And she refused to beg.

Summoning her tattered pride, she raised her chin. "Fine. I'll go. You don't need to tell me twice."

Her heart shredded, her hopes obliterated, she turned and walked away.

Chapter 14

Cole tossed down his pen, creaked his chair back, then scowled at the digital clock ticking away the hours on the corner of his desk. One in the morning. By rights he should be oblivious to the world by now. He'd worked himself into exhaustion during that ride through the mountains, fighting off wolves and gunmen, barely surviving a deadly stampede.

But damned if he could sleep.

He dragged his hand down his unshaven face, then rubbed his stinging eyes. He'd spent the past six hours doing ranch business in an attempt to numb his mind— balancing his checkbook, filing his quarterly taxes, filling out the mountain of insurance forms that had accumulated on his desk. But not even that dull work could deaden the sting of Bethany's betrayal or stop the hot, searing anger scorching through him when his traitorous mind wandered to her.

He shoved thoughts of Bethany aside. She was gone. It was over. He refused to think about her again. He'd done what he'd set out to do and had saved his ranch. That was all that mattered to him.

The clock ticked off another minute, and he shot it another scowl. There was no reason for this insomnia. He'd delivered the cattle. He'd made enough money to operate the ranch for another year. He'd lost his foreman and ranch hands, and he couldn't buy Del's land, but at least that secret society hadn't defeated him yet.

But damn... He'd known Kenny Greene since high school. They'd worked together for years. And Rusty... A hollow feeling gouged his chest. He'd never expected him to betray his trust. Or Bethany...

He shoved himself away from the desk with a growl. Determined to forget her, he strode from the study to the great room, then beelined straight to the bar.

The huge, vaulted room was draped in darkness. His father sat in an armchair by the fireplace, watching the flickering flat-screen television with the sound muted. He looked up, then lumbered to his feet as Cole took out a bottle of Scotch and poured himself a drink.

"Can't sleep?" he asked, joining him at the bar.

Cole knocked back a slug of scotch, felt the fiery burn sear his gut. "I'm not used to the quiet, I guess."

"Sorry about that. I guess I've caused a ruckus the last few weeks."

He shrugged and refilled his glass. "I'll adjust." He always did. He'd bury himself in his ranch work and concentrate on what mattered most—his land.

His father topped off his own glass with his favorite Maker's Mark whiskey, then paused. "Listen, Cole. I know it's not my place to say anything, but about that woman, Bethany..."

Cole flinched. "There's nothing to say."

"I think there is." He paused. "I'd like to give you some advice."

"Advice? From you?" Cole snorted in disbelief. "After all those mistresses?"

His father winced. "I've been a bad example, I know. Your mother…she didn't deserve what I did."

"You got that right." He slopped more Scotch in his glass, then gulped it down with a hiss.

"I just don't want you to make my mistakes."

"I'm not making a mistake. It's over. There's nothing else to say." And he didn't need his father—the man who'd disappointed his family for decades—trying to give *him* relationship advice.

His father stared at his tumbler with a furrowed brow. "For what it's worth, I'm not proud of what I did. I took your mother for granted. All those years…I only thought about myself."

He met Cole's eyes. "The thing is, the fame, the power—none of that mattered in the end. Your mother and our marriage did. But I didn't figure that out until it was too late. And Bethany—"

"It's not the same thing."

"You're sure? It looked like it from where I stood."

"I'm sure." Cole's thoughts veered to Bethany, and his anger flared. "Look, she lied to me. She concealed evidence about the attacks. And the last thing I need is someone I can't depend on. I had enough of that crap growing up."

His father blanched. "I deserve that. I was a miserable father, I know. But I still say you're making a mistake."

"No, I'm not. And I definitely don't need your advice."

His father nodded. He drained his glass, then set it down on the bar. And in that moment he didn't look like the swaggering, bigger-than-life senator who'd wielded so much power. He looked like a tired, middle-aged man—his lined face haggard, his blue eyes filled with remorse.

"You're a lot like me," he finally said, his voice subdued. "Sometimes when I see you, it's like looking back thirty years. I used to think that was a good thing." His mouth twisted into a bitter smile. "But now I know it's a curse."

He turned, his broad shoulders slumped, his steps weary as he left the room. Cole watched him go, denials crowding his throat. His father was wrong. They were nothing alike. He felt insulted at the thought.

And his father was dead wrong about Bethany. She'd had her chance, and she'd let him down, just as she had in the past.

He started to top off his glass, then stopped. What the hell. He'd take the whole damned bottle to bed. Maybe then he could finally forget about Bethany and find the oblivion he sought.

By morning, Cole knew two things with absolute clarity. Getting drunk solved nothing, and hangovers were a bitch.

His head pounding, his stomach lurching like a fly-fishing line during a spawning run, he jerked open his blurry eyes. Sunlight stabbed his brain. The bedroom heaved and twirled, the stench of whiskey souring the air.

He rolled over, causing a thousand hammers to flay his skull. Groaning, he forced himself to a sitting position, then gripped his throbbing head to make sure it wouldn't split.

Moving as if he'd aged a hundred years, he pushed himself to his feet, staggered to the master bathroom, then grabbed a handful of painkillers and washed them down.

He glanced in the mirror, his bloodshot eyes and rumpled clothes proof that he'd hit a new low.

And what was worse, even all that alcohol hadn't enabled him to avoid the truth—that Bethany had had a point.

Hell. He braced his hands on the vanity and released a breath. He'd seen the way Tony had acted. He knew why she couldn't stay. He even understood why she refused to accuse her father of any wrongdoing without proof. In her place, he would have done the same.

That thought rankling, he stripped off his reeking clothes and stepped into the shower. But while the hot water eased the ache from his muscles and helped clear the fog from his mind, it did nothing to assuage his guilt.

Not that it mattered. Whether he'd been fair to Bethany or not, she was always going to leave. There was nothing for her in Maple Cove. Their argument might have hastened her departure, but she'd never intended to stay.

He flicked off the tap, dried himself with a towel, and pulled on a clean T-shirt and jeans. Feeling marginally more human, he headed down the hallway to the kitchen, hoping a mug of strong, black coffee would jump-start his sluggish brain.

Ace padded over and whined. Still moving carefully, Cole bent to rub his ears. "What's up, buddy? Did everyone leave us alone today?"

Straightening, he glanced around the empty great room. The deep silence permeating the house indicated that he was alone. Good. He didn't feel like explaining his hangover to his father. It would only prove his point.

He started toward the kitchen, honing in on the scent of coffee like a desert survivor spotting a lake. But Ace perked up his ears and yipped, then trotted to the front door.

"Great." A visitor before he'd had a shot of caffeine. He

detoured toward the door with a sigh. It was probably the sheriff, getting back to him with the latest news.

But when he was halfway there, the telephone rang. He paused, torn, but the shrill sound jackhammering his skull decided the choice. Desperate to stop the racket, he lunged for the phone. "Bar Lazy K."

"Cole? This is Caitlin. Caitlin O'Donahue. Remember me?"

"Sure." His sister's best friend was hard to forget with her fiery red hair and impressive brains—not to mention her centerfold curves. He rubbed his aching head. "How are you doing? I thought you were in South America doing the Doctors Without Borders thing."

"I was. I just got back. I heard about Lana's kidnapping on the news. I still can't believe it. It's so awful! Have you heard anything more?"

"Not really." Nothing he could reveal.

"How's your mother holding up?"

"About how you'd imagine. Not great."

"She must be devastated."

"You should call her. She'd appreciate hearing from you."

"I will." She hesitated. "If there's anything I can do, will you let me know? I mean it, Cole. I'll do anything, fly anywhere… She might…" Her voice trembled. "She might need a friendly face when this is done. I'm staying at my dad's house in California, so you can reach me here."

"Thanks, Caitlin. I'll pass that on." He hung up the phone, experiencing a sliver of warmth. At least his sister had a loyal friend. His mind instantly flashed to Bethany, but he grimly fought it down. He was not going down that futile track.

Ace pawed at the door and whined, then gave him a reproachful look. "Sorry. *Sorry*," he said. Sending a longing glance toward the kitchen—and that desperately needed caffeine—he closed the distance to the front door. As soon as he cracked it open, Ace bolted out, stopping to sniff a small flat package by the steps.

Cole's pulse skipped. It was a cardboard mailer, the type that held CDs. He scanned the deserted yard, but whoever had delivered it was gone.

He snapped his gaze back to the mailer. An ominous feeling crept through his nerves. *Damn.* With Kenny Greene out of the picture, he'd hoped for a reprieve.

His dread rising, he scooped up the package, and returned to the house. Just as he expected, the mailer held a DVD. He crossed the room, slid it into the DVD player, and turned it on.

The screen flickered to life. A room swirled dizzily into view. He closed his eyes, cursing that bottle of Scotch. But the unsteadiness was due to the photographer, who couldn't quite keep the camera still.

The camera swerved to a loveseat. And suddenly, his sister appeared on the screen, and he forgot to breathe. Although the camera continued to bobble, he could see her clearly enough—her mussed blond hair, the harsh pallor of her face, the exhaustion in her scared blue eyes. She perched on a white loveseat, clutching a piece of paper in her shaking hands.

His face burned. Blood thundered through his skull. And he trembled with the need to avenge her, to lash out and beat her captors, to charge through that television screen and yank her to safety fast.

But he forced himself to breathe, to take note of details instead. The white loveseat with the turquoise pillows. The thick white carpet beneath her feet. The Picasso print behind the sofa, hanging crookedly on the wall. Traffic rumbled faintly in the background. A distant siren wailed. Next to the sofa was a window, filled with autumn leaves.

Lana cleared her throat, then studied the paper, which appeared to be some sort of script. "As you can see, I'm alive," she read, her voice wavering slightly. "And I'll stay that way as long as you cooperate."

She hesitated, sending a look of desperation at someone off camera, the vulnerability in her eyes cracking his heart. Inhaling visibly, she looked at the paper again. "So please, Dad." Her voice broke. "Turn yourself in. It's the only way to…"

She stopped. She bit her lip, then lifted her chin and stared straight into the camera, a dull flush darkening her pale cheeks. And suddenly, a spark lit her eyes, the same gritty determination he'd seen when she was a kid hounding her older brothers, determined not to be left behind.

"Don't do what they say, Daddy!" she blurted out. A man lunged onscreen, his back to the camera, obscuring Cole's view of Lana, but she continued to speak. "They're going to kill me regardless—"

The man swung his arm, and the sickening sound of flesh hitting flesh cut her off. Cole surged toward the screen, his pulse thundering, the urgent need to do violence eroding what little remained of his self-control.

The man moved aside. Lana slumped against the love seat, her lips trembling, her shocked eyes glittering with tears, her dark-red jaw already beginning to swell.

Cole stared at the screen, his breath shallow and fast, every muscle poised to attack. *That man was dead.* If it was the last thing Cole did, he'd make him pay. The man moved away from the camera, and the screen went blank.

Cole had never been more scared in his life.

* * *

Two hours later, the DVD ended for the second time, and a shocked silence gripped the group clustered around the screen. Cole skipped his gaze from the grim-faced sheriff to his ashen father, to his uncle Don and Bonnie Gene. Hannah stood by the kitchen, hugging her orange cat, looking as if she wanted to cry.

His aunt finally broke the silence. "What…" She cleared her throat and tried again. "What are we going to do now?"

"Good question." Donald's voice vibrated with anger. "Maybe Hank has an idea since he got her into this mess. If he hadn't been so self-centered—"

"Lay off him," Cole cut in, surprising himself. "What's done is done. It doesn't do any good to keep blaming him now."

Everyone turned to face him, their mouths agape. He'd never defended his father before. But what was the point of continually hurling blame?

He glanced at his father hunched on the sofa, his face chalk-white, his still-thick hair streaked with gray. He'd aged in the past few weeks, turning into a shell of his former self.

And suddenly, Cole realized he pitied his father. Hank had made mistakes, but he'd received his just due. He'd lost his job, his wife, his prestige. He was a broken, pathetic man who no longer had the power to hurt anyone.

And Cole realized something else. He'd let the bitterness he'd harbored since childhood go.

The sheriff cleared his throat. "I'll take the DVD to the FBI. They'll have a forensic team enhance the images, see if they can figure out the location."

Cole steered his mind to the DVD. "She's back in the United States. In a city." When everyone stared at him, he shrugged. "That siren you hear in the background. It's not a European type. And those leaves on the tree in the window are turning colors, so she's probably somewhere in the north or east. That room is either on the ground level or a lower floor since we can see the tree."

"By God, you're right," his father said. "Good thinking."

The sheriff nodded. "That's exactly the kind of detail that can break this case. With luck, the FBI can pinpoint her location and send in a S.W.A.T. team to get her out."

Conversation broke out around him. But Cole tuned it out, his thoughts still circling around the revelation he'd had. And he realized it was true. He'd finally freed himself from the past, giving up the bitterness that had driven him for years.

But his father's accusation still lingered. Was he really as bad as his dad?

Suddenly feeling restless, he went outside and stood on the porch. He bent to pet Mitzy and Ace, who'd instantly converged on his feet, then looked out over the yard.

Bethany had wronged him. She'd even admitted as much. But he understood why she'd done it, and he couldn't fault her for that. So why couldn't he forgive her? If he'd finally stopped resenting his father after all these years, why not her?

His arms crossed, he frowned at the distant mountains, knowing he was missing something important, something big. She'd left, just as he'd known she would—just as she had before. But had her departure really been inevitable? How would he know if he'd never asked her to stay? And why hadn't he asked? Had he been afraid that she'd say no?

Was he still reliving his childhood, expecting rejection at every turn?

He scowled, not happy with that unflattering insight, but he knew he'd discovered the truth. He'd pushed her away before she could abandon him.

But Bethany would never do that. She'd proven her loyalty time and again. She'd saved his horses from the burning barn. She'd risked her life to stop the stampede. She'd even confronted Tony—the man who'd tormented her for years—to stop the sabotage on his ranch. How much proof of her loyalty did he need?

Hell, he'd been the selfish one. He'd overlooked the bullying. He'd ignored her medical talents, refusing to acknowledge that she'd needed opportunities she couldn't find in Maple Cove.

His chest tight, he gazed out at the ranch he'd worked so hard to attain—the wide-open plains and rolling hills, the rugged mountains covered with snow, the hawks soaring past on the wind. He loved this land. He loved the freedom, the history, the unspoiled beauty that soothed his soul.

But he couldn't ask Bethany to give up her life in Chicago, to sacrifice everything for his sake. He'd resented his father for only thinking about himself. He couldn't do the same to her.

He sighed. This land had always been here. It would be here when he was gone. And while he loved it, he'd used it as a crutch, to give purpose to his angry life.

But he no longer needed it as much as he needed her.

He went dead still. *That* was how he resembled his father. His staunch independence. His refusal to rely on anyone else. But while his father's reluctance to admit he needed help could cost his sister her life, Cole's could cost him his heart.

He strode back into the great room and headed down the hall. "Where are you going?" his father called.

Pausing, Cole glanced at the man who'd sired him, the man he was determined not to become. "I'm taking your advice and buying a plane ticket to Chicago."

To claim the woman he'd always loved.

Chapter 15

Bethany gazed out the taxi window, the bleak gray skies over Lake Shore Drive echoing her gloomy mood. She rarely splurged on a taxi, but a miserable, sleepless night and a raging headache had convinced her to skip the train. The noise from the taxi was bad enough.

They exited the busy highway, then cut across town toward Michigan Avenue, whipping in and out of traffic so fast she could barely keep her seat. An ambulance screamed past. A bus rumbled by, belching a cloud of black exhaust, then screeched to a stop and blocked the road. The taxi driver lay on his horn.

"I'll get out here," Bethany said, her head about to burst. She thrust several bills at the driver and hopped out, the cold breeze whipping her hair. Clutching her coat closer around her, she hurried past the towering high-rise buildings to the Preston-Werner Clinic. She still hadn't heard from Adam, even though she'd left him a voice mail to tell him she'd returned. She'd decided to go straight to the study supervisor instead.

A businessman strode past, and his briefcase banged her leg. "Hey!" She whirled around, but he didn't break his stride. She scowled, wondering when Chicago had changed. She used to love the energy in the city. It made her feel exuberant and alive. Now she just felt annoyed.

She walked through the automatic front doors of the clinic, her heels rapping on the shiny marble floor. Too exhausted to take the stairs, she punched the button for the elevator and stepped inside. Then she leaned back against the wall and watched the numbers of the floors flash past.

Her thoughts instantly arrowed to Cole, an unbearable ache wrenching her throat, but she pushed him out of her mind. She could not go there. Not now, not in a public place. She'd save that agony for later, when she could wallow in her misery alone.

The elevator stopped. She entered the supervisor's office, relieved that the woman had agreed to see her. In her late fifties, Marge Holbrook was a tall, thin woman with a short, no-nonsense haircut that matched her managerial style. Surely she would take Bethany's side.

"Bethany," the supervisor said when she walked in. She nodded to one of the large leather chairs in front of her gleaming desk. "Have a seat."

"Thanks." Bethany sank into the chair. "I appreciate your seeing me. I just got back into town last night. I was hoping we could talk about the information I found."

Marge quirked a well-shaped brow. "What information?"

Bethany's heart skipped. "The dissertation I discovered at Montana State. I emailed Adam a copy, and he promised to pass it on."

"He didn't give me anything."

Uneasiness trickled through her. Why hadn't Adam given her a copy? He'd had plenty of time.

Suddenly, Cole's question popped into her mind. *How well do you know the people you work with?*

Her hand unsteady, she took the flash drive from her purse and slid it across the desk. Maybe she was wrong. Maybe there was another explanation for this.

Or maybe not.

"Mrs. Bolter's death really upset me," she explained. "I *know* I didn't misjudge the dose. So I decided to investigate to see if I could find another cause."

"And did you?"

"Not at first. But I saw she'd been to rehab years ago. That surprised me because she used to bring us rum cake with a glaze that could knock your socks off. You could get drunk on the fumes alone."

Marge cracked a smile. "I had a slice once."

Bethany nodded. "So I went to the library at Montana State and used their database to do some research. Eventually, I came across a study involving a drug similar to Rheumectatan that caused reactions in patients with damaged livers. One of the reactions was sudden cardiac arrest, especially in post-menopausal women like Mrs. Bolter."

The supervisor removed her glasses and placed them on her desk. "The pharmaceutical company would have known all that before the trial began. If the side effect applied to Rheumectatan, it would have come out."

"You're right. It should have come out. But what if it didn't...for whatever reason?"

Marge leaned back in her chair, a fine line creasing her brow. She tapped a finger against her lips for several seconds, then leaned forward again. "Go on."

"I phoned Adam right away and emailed him a copy of the dissertation. He promised to make sure you got it, too. He also said you'd halt the study until you were sure the patients were safe."

Her eyes narrowed. "He didn't mention anything to me."

Bethany closed her eyes. She could no longer ignore the proof. Adam had lied. He'd set her up to take the blame for something she didn't do. *But why?*

She struggled to breathe, the terrible betrayal leaving her raw. "I know I didn't give Mrs. Bolter the wrong dose. There has to be another reason she died."

"The records show you made a mistake."

"They're wrong. Someone must have falsified them."

"The autopsy backed them up."

Bethany's head swam. The autopsy had shown the wrong dose? But how? "I don't know exactly what happened, but there must be an explanation. Adam was working that night. And if he lied about the study…"

"That's quite an accusation."

"So is blaming me for something I didn't do."

Her eyes thoughtful, Marge picked up the flash drive and turned it over in her hand. "I'll call in a forensic computer scientist to check the records. They can tell if anyone tampered with them. I'll need a copy of your plane ticket with the time of your flight. And I'll halt the study until we're sure the patients are safe."

Still reeling, Bethany managed to nod. "Thank you."

"You're still suspended until we investigate this thoroughly," Marge warned.

"I understand."

"And I don't want you mentioning this to anyone. If you're right and someone went to the trouble of falsifying records…"

She could be in terrible danger. "I won't."

She wobbled to her feet, feeling numb. She'd trusted Adam. She considered him her friend. But he'd set her up, tried to incriminate her in the patient's death. And in the process, he'd robbed her of every last illusion she'd had.

Had her deception hurt Cole this badly?

Unable to bear that dreadful thought, she returned to her apartment. She tossed her coat and purse on the sofa, then went to her living room window and gazed down at the busy street. Cars raced past. Skyscrapers loomed around her, blocking her view of the leaden sky. She closed her eyes and pressed her forehead against the cool glass, trying to bring sense to her suddenly shattered world.

Mrs. Bolter had died. That was a fact. She might have suffered a reaction to the drug, which Adam had covered up. But what motive could he possibly have? Did he fear a malpractice suit? But that didn't make sense. No one knew about the potential side effect or even Mrs. Bolter's stint in rehab. So why had he needed to lie?

She shook her head. One thing she *did* know—Cole's aunt Bonnie Gene was right. No one was all good or all bad. Not Adam. Not Cole's father. Not her own father, who was reduced to staying with a friend in town. Not even her.

And she'd learned something else in the past two weeks. There was no perfect place. She'd come to Chicago to reinvent herself, thinking she could break free of stereotypes, that people would see her as herself, not just a member of her race.

But instead of finding freedom, she'd become anonymous and lost, one of millions of unknown people living in a noisy, crowded place.

She turned around and eyed the apartment that had meant so much to her only a short time ago—the Ethan Allen sofa she'd scrimped to buy, the shelves overflowing with books. She realized she could walk away right now and wouldn't miss a single thing, except the coffee table her father had made.

She walked across the carpet to the coffee table, then lowered herself to the couch. She trailed her hand along the smooth oak legs, the satiny wood her father had patiently sanded and stained. She splayed her hands across the top, her gaze lingering on the arrowhead collection arranged beneath the protective glass. And images crowded her mind, a rapid-fire barrage of memories she could no longer stem—riding her horse across the plains with Cole. Hunting for arrowheads together at the teepee ring, his blue eyes crinkling into a smile. Digging side by side beneath the buffalo jump, then rolling together in the grass, laughing and making love.

And suddenly, she understood. The truth had been here all along, literally in front of her face. Her heart wasn't in Chicago. It never had been. She belonged in Montana, just as these arrowheads did. It had just taken her a while to realize that.

Maybe she'd had to leave Montana to escape the prejudice and test her wings in a different place. But her trip home had made her realize that she liked living in Maple Cove. She liked seeing people she knew around town, even if they weren't always ideal. Chicago had great amenities—theaters, museums, amazing shopping and cafés. But she could find those things in Montana, too.

And who was she trying to fool? She could do the work she loved in Montana. There were plenty of clinics and hospitals, including one in Honey Creek. And more importantly, she loved Cole.

But did Cole love her? Did he need her? Would he want her to come back?

Her stomach jittered hard. She squeezed her arms to her chest, trying to quell the attack of nerves. She thought back to that night in the mountains and the tender way he'd made love, and the answer hit her upside the head. *Of course* he loved her. He wouldn't have reacted with such fury to her deception if he hadn't cared.

But he didn't trust her—and why should he? She'd deceived him about her father. She'd run out on him twice. If she wanted a future with him she had to prove that she'd stick around.

She nibbled her lip, suddenly uncertain—because her father was right about something else. She didn't like to reveal any weakness. Maybe it was because she'd grown up around cowboys. Or maybe it had begun with Tony, who'd thrived on inciting her fear. Whatever the cause, she never showed any vulnerability or risked her heart.

But it was time to start. If her father had sacrificed his home for her mother, she could bend her pride for the man she loved.

She jumped to her feet and rushed to the phone in the kitchen, creating lists in her mind. She had to call and resign her job. She had to arrange for a moving company to ship her coffee table and books. She could fit her clothes in a couple of suitcases and donate the rest to a charity, along with her dishes and bed.

A knock sounded at the door.

Her thoughts instantly leaped to Cole.

But that was ridiculous. He wasn't in Chicago. It was probably her neighbor dropping off the mail.

Trying to hold back her burgeoning hopes, she hurried to the door. She peeked out the peephole, but no one came into view—which was odd. Unless her neighbor had simply left the mail on the floor...

Her pulse accelerating, she put her ear to the door. Silence. She dithered, the Raven Head Society's threat springing to mind. But that was silly. They had no reason to harm her now. And the hall appeared empty from what she could see. Making a face at her imagination, she slipped off the chain and peered out.

The door flew open and slammed against her. Crying out, she stumbled back. A man muscled his way inside, knocking her to her knees. Startled, she scrambled back up.

"Adam."

He stood between her and the door, his eyes wild, his breathing ragged and loud. His face was flushed, his normally meticulous blond hair awry. He wore one of his usual tailored suits, indicating he'd just finished his morning rounds.

Her mind whirled frantically through options. He couldn't know that she'd talked to the supervisor. Marge wouldn't have let that slip. So if she could just bluff her way through...

"You startled me." Did her voice sound too high? She struggled to tone it down while her pulse went berserk. "I'm glad you stopped by, though. Do you have time to talk? You wouldn't believe all the things I went through in Montana—even a stampede."

Afraid she was starting to ramble, she turned toward the kitchen, her gaze darting to the phone. But a click stopped her dead in her tracks.

"Not so fast."

She slowly turned to face him. A gun had appeared in his hand. And dread pooled deep in her gut. "What... What's this about?"

"As if you don't know." His hand trembled. His Adam's apple dipped, betraying his unease. So he didn't like handling a weapon. If she could keep him talking and find a way to distract him...

"You weren't supposed to survive that attack," he said.

"Attack?" She blinked, not needing to feign her confusion now. "You mean those men in the mountains? But how did you—"

"Mountains? No. In Bozeman. That idiot watched the ranch for days, waiting for a chance to get you alone, and he still didn't get it right."

The truck that tried to run her off the road. "That was you?"

"Not me. A man I hired."

"But why? Why would you want to hurt me? I thought we were friends."

A flush darkened his face. His gun wobbled, and guilt flashed through his eyes. "I didn't want to hurt you, but I had no choice. It was the only way I could get that drug approved after Mrs. Bolter died."

"The drug? But what…"

"Why do you think? I need the money. I've got medical-school loans up to my ears. Rhyne-tex promised me a bonus if I got it approved. And I invested in their stock, so I'll make a bundle there, too."

The pharmaceutical company had bribed him? "But that's illegal."

He laughed. "Oh, come on, Bethany. You can't be that naive. Everyone does it—professors, medical-school boards, doctors… Drugs are big business. There are billions of dollars involved. There's no reason I can't take a cut."

She stared at him, unable to believe she'd misjudged him so badly. How could she have considered him a friend? "So you'll sacrifice your patients for money."

"No one was supposed to die. I thought the drug was safe."

"But it's not safe. Mrs. Bolter died. How can you let them approve it after that?"

"They can pull it off the market later. I only need to get it approved. I'll get my bonus. I'll sell off my stocks and make a mint. I don't care what happens after that."

Her anger rose. "So you set me up to take the blame."

"I had to. I couldn't risk that they'd stop the study. Not when we're so close."

"But—"

"I told you. I can't let them stop that trial." His eyes turned hard, and he raised the gun. "Even if you have to die."

Chapter 16

Bethany stared down the barrel of the gun, stark fear slithering down her spine. She took in the tremor of Adam's hand, the desperation in his crazed eyes. Every cell in her body went numb.

"It won't do any good," she said. "I've talked to Marge. She already knows what you did."

His eyes flickered with uncertainty, and she forged on. "I gave her the dissertation this morning, just before you came. I told her you changed the records. She's calling in a forensic computer scientist to investigate it now."

He shook his head. Perspiration broke out on his brow. "I don't believe you. You're lying."

"I'm not lying. It's the truth. Call her and ask. I tell you, I was just there."

His gun wobbled. His face turned a sickening gray. She transferred her weight to the balls of her feet, ready to leap his way.

But he narrowed his eyes and steadied his aim. "It's too late. I'm in too deep. If I'm going down, so are you."

Panic broke free inside her. She couldn't die. She had too much to live for. She had to stop him—but how?

Her head light, her pulse frenzied, she struggled to think through the fear. "Listen, Adam. Let's think this out. There's no need for you to—"

The doorbell buzzed. Adam's eyes flew to the door.

Bethany didn't hesitate. She lunged to his side and grabbed his wrist. He whipped up his arm, his strength catching her off-balance, and it was all she could do to hang on.

The gun went off. Ceiling plaster rained down, the sulfuric smell of gunpowder filling the air. Her ears ringing from the gunshot, she clung to his arm, struggling to wrest the weapon from his iron grip.

But desperation had lent him strength. He turned and slammed her against the wall. She cried out, trying to stay upright and gouged his arm with her nails. The door burst open, but she ignored it. Adam rammed her back even harder, bringing tears of pain to her eyes.

She kneed his groin. He let out a howl of outrage, then twisted and flung her aside. She fell to the floor, pain shooting through her knees and arms, panic pounding her brain. She whipped up her head, then froze, caught in the crosshairs of Adam's gun.

Triumph lit his eyes. A wild sound formed in her throat. And she knew in that instant that she would die.

But a man barreled out of nowhere and tackled Adam. The pistol went off again. The two men wrestled to the floor, grappling for supremacy, and Bethany leaped out of their way.

The man slammed his fist into Adam's face. Adam

cried out and loosened his grip. The gun skittered across the floor, and Bethany rushed to pick it up.

Her pulse going berserk, she whirled around and aimed. The newcomer turned, and she glimpsed his face. *Cole.* But how...?

She gave her head a hard shake, forcing the distraction aside. She circled the men, trying to get a clear shot at Adam, but he was still fighting, moving too fast for her to see.

More fists flew. The men grunted and rolled, crashing against the table and scattering chairs. Adam was strong, but no match for Cole, who'd worked for years on the ranch. Cole jumped to his feet and drew back his fist, putting the power of his steel-hard body behind it, then unleashed the explosive punch. A sickening thud rent the air. Adam crumpled, unconscious, on the floor.

Her heart rioting, Bethany kept the gun trained on Adam as Cole straightened and stepped away. But there was no need. He'd knocked Adam out cold.

Cole tugged off his belt, flipped Adam over, and secured his arms. Then he lurched to his feet and turned to face her, his breath loud in the silent room. She clicked on the safety and slowly lowered the gun.

His eyes met hers. Her lips quivered, the terror finally penetrating the adrenaline surge. Cole strode over, took the gun from her hand and set it on the table, then dragged her into his arms.

Her knees went weak. She clung to his massive shoulders, unable to believe he was really here. He'd saved her. If he hadn't shown up, she would have died.

Tremors wracked her body. Hot tears sprang to her eyes. She held him close, giving herself over to his power and strength, wanting to crawl right into his skin.

"Who the hell is that?" he asked, his voice rough against her ear.

"Adam. The doctor I work with. He set me up…" Her voice broke.

"Shhh." Cole tightened his hold, burying her face against his neck. "Don't talk now. I'll hear the story later when you tell the police."

Still trembling, she wiped her eyes on her sleeve and looked up. "Oh, God, Cole…" Her voice cracked. "If you hadn't…"

"It's all right. It's over."

Thanks to him.

Bethany was still struggling to gather her composure a short time later after the police had taken their statements and hauled her coworker away. She turned to Cole, overcome with a myriad of conflicting emotions—shock, longing, relief—and dragged in a shuddering breath. As horrific as that ordeal had been, it wasn't finished yet. Cole had saved her life, rescuing her from Adam's attack. But the next few minutes would determine her future—and whether it would be with him.

Afraid to hope, but needing desperately to know the answer, she stepped closer and met his eyes. "Cole…why are you here?"

He reached out and tipped up her chin. His solemn blue eyes held hers. "I couldn't let you go. I love you. I always have. I wanted to beg you for another chance."

Beg *her?* More tears flooded her eyes. She bit down hard on her lip, fearing if she let herself cry she wouldn't stop. He loved her. He was willing to give her a chance. "You forgive me for lying to you?"

His thumb stroked her jaw, regret filling his eyes. "Forgive you? I'm the one who needs forgiveness."

"But—"

"I love you, Bethany. I always have. But I was too scared, too caught up in the past to understand—to really see what you needed to do. And I blamed you for things that weren't your fault."

Her heart wrenched. Tears tracked down her cheek. "I love you, too, Cole. In all these years, I've never stopped."

He gazed at her with an expression so loving, so filled with wonderment that her throat closed up, and her heart nearly burst from her chest.

He gently cradled her head as if she were the most precious being on earth. And then he lowered his mouth to hers and kissed her until her head swam, the shivers eased from her body, and reality faded away.

After an eternity, he ended the kiss and hugged her against his heart, exactly where she wanted to be—surrounded by his strength, his tenderness, his love.

"I'll move here," he said.

Startled, she pulled back and searched his eyes. "But your ranch…"

"I like it there," he admitted. "But I need you more than I need the land. I'll go wherever you want, as long as you'll marry me."

She couldn't breathe. "You'd sacrifice your ranch for me?"

"We can go there on vacations, maybe retire there someday. Your father can manage it while we're gone."

"My father?" Her world tilted again. "But you fired him. He lied to you about those men."

Cole let out a heavy sigh. "Yeah, he lied. He made mistakes. He got in over his head, then tried to protect you from those goons. But I haven't been perfect, either. I've already hired him back."

Stunned, she shook her head. "I don't want you to leave

the ranch. I love it there, too. I want to come back to Montana to be with you. There's nothing for me in Chicago. I figured that out before you came."

"You're sure? Because I don't mind—"

"I'm sure, Cole. Maybe I had to get away at first. I had to learn that there is no perfect place, that there are good and bad people everywhere. But I'm ready to come home now. To be with you."

His eyes held hers. He pulled away slightly, then tugged a small velvet box from his pocket and held it out.

Her breath backed up. She met his eyes, more tears swimming in her eyes. "Cole…"

"Take it," he whispered.

Her hands trembling, she took the box and flipped it open. A brilliant diamond ring winked back.

"You'll marry me?" he asked, his deep voice cracking.

Her knees wobbled. Emotions crowded inside her—wonder, joy, love. She slid the ring on, then clenched her fingers, hardly able to see him through her tears. "I'll marry you."

His lips took hers, and a feeling of absolute *rightness* flooded her heart. She'd marry Cole. She'd raise their children in Montana, where her roots were, alongside the man she'd always loved.

Where she knew that she belonged.

Epilogue

Senator Hank Kelley stood in the great room at the Bar Lazy K ranch, staring out the windows at the snow-covered fields. The ranch had quieted down over the last few days, but the lull only heightened his nerves. He knew the calm gripping the ranch was deceptive. Those killers were still out there—plotting, watching, biding their time…

And if he didn't do something fast, Lana would die.

He shuddered hard. Seeing his daughter on that DVD had shaken him badly. Her terrified eyes haunted him day and night. Hell, he was so wound up he couldn't sleep, couldn't eat, could barely hold on to a thought.

His cell phone rang, and he jumped, experiencing a sickening spurt of dread. His pulse chaotic, he pulled out his phone and stared at the unknown number. The police? The kidnappers? The secret society?

Feeling light-headed, he clicked it on.

"Senator Hank Kelley?" a woman asked.

"You're talking to him."

"Hold the line, please. President Colton would like to speak to you."

The president. Hank's heart sank. The FBI must have told him about the assassination plot. Colton would be furious. He'd want Hank's resignation—or worse.

"Senator Kelley?" President Colton barked out.

"Yes, sir. It's me. I…" Excuses leaped to his tongue, but he managed to bite them back. "Are you all right?" he asked instead.

"Of course I'm all right. I'll be damned if I'll let a bunch of thugs intimidate me. My reforms are going through, no matter what."

Hank's breath came out in a rush. "I'm glad, sir. I never had anything to do with that plot. I…I hope you realize that."

"That's for the police to decide. In the meantime, I recommend you resign."

Hank's stomach nosedived. He'd lost the president's trust—and rightly so. "Yes, sir. I'll do that right away."

"See that you do." The president hung up.

Hank put away his phone, then stared blankly out the window, his mind numb, a hollow ache filling his gut. It was over. He'd screwed up too many times. His children despised him. His wife was going to divorce him. The career he'd spent his life building had finally come crashing down.

The irony of it struck him hard. President Colton worked for the good of the country. Hank had only worked for the good of himself. And where had it gotten him? Colton was popular and respected; he had an adoring wife—while Hank's marriage and career had failed.

His half brother, Donald, emerged from the kitchen and

joined him at the window. Hank stood silently beside him, unable to think of a thing to say.

"Who called?" Donald finally asked.

Hank exhaled. There was no point hiding the truth. "The president. He asked me to resign."

Donald didn't answer. Several long minutes passed. Hank continued looking out the window at the demolished barn, a fitting symbol of his ruined life.

Then Cole and Bethany came into view, leading their horses past the rubble. They stopped near the porch, laughing about something Hank couldn't hear. Then Cole tugged her close and kissed her. He didn't stop for a very long time.

A wistful feeling unfolded inside Hank, a sense of loss. He'd had a love like that once, and he'd thrown it away. But at least his son wouldn't make his mistakes. He'd found the happiness he deserved.

He cleared his throat, then turned to face his brother. "You know…I never thanked you. For stepping in and taking care of Cole when you did. You did a damned good job with him, better than I could have done."

Donald's steady gaze met his. After a moment, he dipped his head. "Cole's a good man."

His chest thick, Hank turned his gaze back to the window again. Donald had acknowledged his apology. It didn't solve the problems between them, but it was a start.

Cole leaped on his horse. Bethany did the same. Still laughing, their faces bright with the promise of love, they loped away.

Hank stood beside his brother and watched them go. He'd been a wretched father, no doubt about that. And he'd rightfully paid the price. But he still had a chance to do something right by saving his daughter's life.

He couldn't take action yet. The FBI wouldn't let him

leave the ranch. But he would watch and wait. And then act when the time was right.

Even if he had to die.

* * * * *

So you think you can write?

**Mills & Boon® and Harlequin®
have joined forces in a
global search for new authors.**

It's our biggest contest yet—with the prize
of being published by the world's
leader in romance fiction.

In September join us for our unique
Five Day Online Writing Conference
www.soyouthinkyoucanwrite.com

Meet 50+ romance editors who want to
buy your book and get ready to
submit your manuscript!

So you think you can write?
Show us!

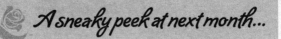

A sneaky peek at next month...

INTRIGUE...

BREATHTAKING ROMANTIC SUSPENSE

My wish list for next month's titles...

In stores from 21st September 2012:

☐ Colby Law – Debra Webb

& At His Command – Karen Anders

☐ Spy Hard & The Spy Wore Spurs
   – Dana Marton

☐ Cavanaugh Rules – Marie Ferrarella

& It Started That Night – Virna DePaul

☐ Rancher Under Cover – Carla Cassidy

Available at WHSmith, Tesco, Asda, Eason, Amazon and Apple

Just can't wait?

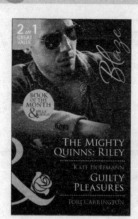

Special Offers

Every month we put together collections and longer reads written by your favourite authors.

Here are some of next month's highlights— and don't miss our fabulous discount online!

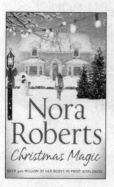

Nora Roberts
Christmas Magic

OVER 400 MILLION OF HER BOOKS IN PRINT WORLDWIDE

On sale 5th October

Gift-Wrapped **GOVERNESSES**

Sophia James
Annie Burrows
Marguerite Kaye

Three Regency Christmas romances

On sale 5th October

PENNY JORDAN COLLECTION
Mediterranean nights

OVER 100 MILLION BOOKS SOLD WORLDWIDE

On sale 5th October

Save 20% on all Special Releases

Find out more at
www.millsandboon.co.uk/specialreleases

Visit us Online

1012/ST/MB38

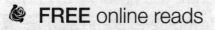

The World of Mills & Boon®

There's a Mills & Boon® series that's perfect for you. We publish ten series and, with new titles every month, you never have to wait long for your favourite to come along.

Scorching hot, sexy reads
4 new stories every month

By Request

Relive the romance with the best of the best
9 new stories every month

Romance to melt the heart every time
12 new stories every month

Desire™

Passionate and dramatic love stories
8 new stories every month

Have Your Say

You've just finished your book.
So what did you think?

We'd love to hear your thoughts on our
'Have your say' online panel
www.millsandboon.co.uk/haveyoursa

- 🌹 Easy to use
- 🌹 Short questionnaire
- 🌹 Chance to win Mills & Boon® goodies

YOUR_SA